What the Millionaire Wants...

METSY HINGLE

MILLS & BOON®
Pure reading pleasure™

First published in Great Britain 2009
Large Print edition 2009
Harlequin Mills & Boon Limited,
Eton House, 18-24 Paradise Road,
Richmond, Surrey TW9 1SR

© Metsy Hingle 2008

ISBN: 978 0 263 20998 3

Set in Times Roman 16½ on 19 pt.
36-0609-49557

Printed and bound in Great Britain
by CPI Antony Rowe, Chippenham, Wiltshire

METSY HINGLE

is an award-winning, bestselling author of series and single title romantic suspense novels. Metsy is known for creating powerful and passionate stories and her own life reads like a romance novel—from her early years in a New Orleans orphanage and foster care to her long, happy marriage to her husband, Jim, and the rearing of their four children. She recently traded in her business suits and fast-paced life in the hotel and public-relations arena to pursue writing full-time. Metsy loves hearing from readers. For a free bookmark write to Metsy at PO Box 3224, Covington, LA 70433, USA or visit her website at www.metsyhingle.com

For the city of New Orleans and its people who continue to inspire me

One

"**I** am not for sale, Mr. Hawke."

Jackson Hawke bit back a smile as he stared at the woman across the desk. "I'm not trying to buy you, Ms. Spencer. I'm merely offering to employ you."

"I already have a job," she informed him with the cool disdain of a true Southern belle. "I'm the general manager of the Contessa Hotel."

He had to give her points for moxie, Jack thought. He had expected any number of reactions to the news that he had acquired the defaulted bank loan on the small New Orleans hotel. He had made a career of taking over financially troubled companies, revamping them and turning the once-failing operations into profit centers. In each case, his presence was seldom welcome. More often than not his arrival was met with trepidation or anger, and in some cases both. He had expected no less from the owners of the Contessa Hotel. What he hadn't anticipated was defiance. And *defiant* was the only way to describe the woman seated across from him. Unfortunately for Ms. Laura Jordan Spencer, her defiance didn't change the fact that he now owned her family's hotel. "True. But given the circumstances, your position here could prove to be temporary," he countered.

"There is nothing temporary about my position here, Mr. Hawke," she advised him, a hint of temper coloring her voice. "My great grandfather built this hotel nearly a hundred years ago and it's been owned by the Jordan family ever since. I'm sorry if you were led to believe that we would consider selling the property. But I can assure you, the Contessa is *not* for sale."

"I have a receipt for fifteen million dollars that says otherwise," he told her.

"Which I'm sure the bank will refund you once I've straightened out this…this misunderstanding."

He leaned forward, met her gaze. "Take another look at those documents, Ms. Spencer," he said, motioning toward the packet of legal papers he'd presented her, which outlined his acquisition of the hotel via her mother's defaulted bank loan. "There *is* no misunderstanding. Hawke Industries now owns this hotel."

Anger flared in her green eyes. "I don't care what those papers say. I'm telling you there's been a mistake," she insisted and punched the button on the intercom. "Penny, try Mr. Benton at the bank again."

"You're wasting your time," he told her. He already knew from his meeting with the bank chairman the previous afternoon that the man had left town that morning.

"The only one wasting my time, Mr. Hawke, is you," she fired back.

While she waited for her assistant to place the call, Jack used the opportunity to study her more closely. He noted the almond-shaped eyes, the stubborn chin, the smooth skin and lush mouth. She wasn't classically beautiful or slap-you-in-the-face sexy. But there was something about her, a sensuality that simmered beneath the all-business exterior. Judging by the quelling look she shot him, his appraisal hadn't gone unnoticed. Nor had it been appreciated.

At the buzz of the intercom, she grabbed the phone. "Yes. I see," she said. "Thank you, Penny."

"Still not available, I take it," he remarked when she hung up the phone.

"He and his family have left for the Thanksgiving holiday. His office is trying to reach him. When they do, I'll get this mess straightened out."

"Talking with Benton isn't going to change the facts, Ms. Spencer. Your mother pledged this hotel as collateral on a loan and Hawke Industries purchased that note, along with several others, from the bank. Since your mother defaulted on that loan, the Contessa Hotel now belongs to Hawke Industries."

"I'm telling you, you're wrong," she insisted. "There is no way my mother would have ever pledged the Contessa."

Tiring of her refusal to accept the obvious, Jack snatched the stack of legal documents, pulled out the collateral mortgage note signed by her mother and slapped it in front of her. "Look at it," he commanded. "That's a promissory note signed by your mother, pledging her stock in the Contessa as guarantee on the loan. Are you going to deny that's her signature?"

Something flickered in her eyes as she stared at the damning document. For the first time since he'd arrived and introduced himself to her as the hotel's new owner, the lady looked uncertain. Just as quickly it was gone and the defiance was back. "I don't care what that says. Even if my mother had wanted to use the hotel as collateral for a loan, she couldn't have."

"And why is that?"

"Because my sister and I each own ten percent

of the hotel's stock. And neither of us would ever consent to her using the hotel."

"She wouldn't have needed your consent—not to pledge her own stock. Which is exactly what she did," he pointed out.

"My mother would never do such a thing. Not without telling me first."

There was something in her voice, a hint of uncertainty. There was also a flicker of fear in her eyes. It was that fear that stirred something inside him. "Didn't you say your mother was out of the country on business?"

She nodded. "She and her husband are opening a nightclub in France."

"Well, maybe she meant to tell you, but just never got around to it," he offered, surprising himself with this sudden surge of empathy. He frowned. Emotion was something he never allowed to enter into his business dealings. It was his own cardinal rule. In the dozens of takeovers he'd engineered, no amount of tears, pleas or offers of sexual favors had deterred him from his course.

"She *has* been busy getting ready for the grand opening."

But he could tell from the lack of conviction in Laura's voice that she didn't believe that telling her about the loan had slipped her mother's mind any more than he did. He had learned firsthand that when it came to money and sex—blood was no thicker than water. Apparently, Deirdre Jordan Spencer Vincenzo Spencer Baxter Arnaud had sold her daughter's legacy and hadn't bothered to inform her of what she'd done.

"At any rate, if, and I'm not saying that she did, but if my mother did pledge her shares of the Contessa as collateral on a loan, I'm sure she didn't understand exactly what that entailed," she told him.

Her stubborn denial sobered him. Shaking off his uncharacteristic spurt of compassion, Jack reminded himself that this was business. Sentiment had no place in business. He didn't intend to let a pretty face, a great pair of legs and a mountain of attitude deter him from his plan. "Or perhaps your mother understood exactly what pledging the hotel as collateral meant."

She stiffened. "Just what is it you're implying, Mr. Hawke?"

"I'm not implying anything, Ms. Spencer. I'm simply pointing out that if your mother had wanted to sell the hotel, but knew you would be opposed to it, using it as collateral on a loan and then defaulting on that loan would be a means of accomplishing her goal."

"How dare you!"

"Why don't we skip the outrage, Ms. Spencer. You strike me as a smart woman. Don't tell me it hasn't crossed your mind. Your mother isn't interested in this place. Why else would she have dumped it in your lap and left the country? Not that I blame her. The hotel was barely breaking even when your grandfather was alive. Since his death, it's been losing money steadily."

She narrowed her eyes suspiciously. "I won't waste my breath asking where you got your information." Temper laced her voice causing the trace of a Southern accent she bore to be more pronounced. "But apparently your source doesn't have all the facts. If he or she did, they would have informed you that the hotel has shown a steady improvement over the past four months. Whatever difficulties the Contessa may have had in the past, they're over. The hotel is doing just fine now."

"Showing a slim profit on last month's financial statement is a long way from being fine."

"I—"

Jack held up his hand. "I'm aware of what you've done since you took over the management six months ago. But you and I both know that this hotel is in need of major upgrades. I intend to see that it not only survives, but that it dominates the small luxury hotel market in this area." He paused, then pressed his point home, saying, "Since you own ten percent of the hotel's stock and are familiar with its operations, I'm willing to allow you to be a part of those plans. Or not. It's your choice. Either way, I'm prepared to make you and your sister both a fair offer for your stock."

"I'm not interested in selling my stock. And neither is my sister."

"Don't be too hasty, Ms. Spencer. After all, you haven't heard my offer yet. And neither has your sister."

"I don't need to hear it. I don't—"

"I'll give you and your sister each two million dollars for your stock. And—"

"I'm not interested."

"Please, do allow me to finish," he said pointedly and noted the angry color flooding her cheeks. "In addition, I'm willing to offer you a management contract with the Contessa at a substantial increase in salary. A salary, which, I might add, is far greater than the one you earned when you were working for the Stratton Hotel group or the Windsor," he added, mentioning the two hotels where his research revealed she had held positions previously.

She hiked up her chin a notch. "Perhaps you should have your hearing checked, Mr. Hawke. As I've already told you, I'm not for sale and neither is the Contessa."

But before he could point out that he already owned the majority of the hotel's stock, there was a tap at the door. "I'm sorry to interrupt, Laura," the perky brunette assistant who had ushered him into the office earlier said from the doorway.

"It's okay, Penny. What is it?"

"You're needed downstairs." She looked over at him, then back at her boss. "You know, for that meeting you scheduled with the kitchen staff."

"Thank you, Penny. Tell them I'm on my way."

Jack didn't miss the look that passed between the two women before her assistant retreated. He suspected it wasn't a meeting that required Laura Spencer's immediate presence. More than likely it was another crisis, one of the many that had plagued the hotel in recent years. As beautiful as the Contessa was and the potential profit she would generate for Hawke Industries, age had taken its toll on the structure. The hotel would continue to deteriorate unless it underwent the necessary maintenance and upgrades it so sorely needed. He intended to see that the hotel was returned to its former glory and became profitable—with or without Laura Spencer's coop-eration.

She stood. "As you heard, I'm late for a meeting, Mr. Hawke. So this discussion is over."

It wasn't often that he found himself so clearly dismissed and certainly not by someone who was in no position to call the shots. A part of him was annoyed. While another part of him couldn't help but admire her spirit. Standing, Jack adjusted his gray suit coat. "I suggest you call your attorneys, Ms. Spencer, and have them review the documents I gave you."

"I intend to."

"Once you've confirmed that Hawke Industries is now the majority stockholder of the Contessa Hotel, I want to meet with you to discuss the hotel's operations. Preferably, tomorrow morning."

"I won't be available tomorrow morning," she informed him.

"Then the afternoon. Two o'clock okay with you?"

"I'll be tied up then, too."

Jack stared at her. Once again, he was surprised by her defiance. His name alone had struck fear in the hearts of many a hardened CEO. Apparently, that wasn't the case with Laura Spencer. He liked the fact that she wasn't afraid of him. And he wasn't averse to the rest of the package, either, he admitted. Under different circumstances he might have entertained the idea of something more personal with her. While he didn't consider himself to have a specific type, he enjoyed the company of intelligent, attractive women. He knew from her education and work history that Laura Spencer was smart. With her big eyes, soft skin and hair that was some shade between red and brown, she certainly was attractive. The perfect package really—except for her connection to the hotel deal. It was that connection that was the problem. Regardless of how attractive he found her on a personal level, he had no intention of letting it get in the way of business. Reminding himself of the business at hand, he said, "Tomorrow evening then. We can discuss my plans for the hotel over dinner."

"I already have plans," she told him.

The intercom buzzed. "Laura, they *really* need you for that meeting."

"I'm on my way," she said. "I have to go."

"I don't suppose there's any point in suggesting another day or time because you'll be tied up then, too," he stated, knowing full well what she was doing. If she agreed to a meeting with him, then she would, in effect, be admitting that everything he had told her was true. Her family no longer owned the Contessa Hotel.

"How perceptive of you, Mr. Hawke. As a matter of fact, my entire week is full and I won't have a moment to spare."

"Then I suggest you make time, Ms. Spencer. Because like it or not, you are going to have to deal with me." And without waiting for her to respond, Jack turned and exited the office.

As she left the hotel's kitchen, Laura pressed her fingers to her temple. The splitting headache that had started with the arrival of Jackson Hawke earlier was quickly working its way toward a migraine. Nodding to various hotel employees, she made her way across the lobby to the elevators. At least her temperamental chef's latest emergency—table salt being substituted for kosher salt—had been fixed relatively easily. She'd simply borrowed some kosher salt from a neighboring restaurant so Chef André could finish his masterpiece. Then she had dispatched one of the busboys to the supply house to swap the incorrectly delivered salt. While the celebrity chef she had hired away from a major restaurant caused her a few hassles, the income he generated by keeping the hotel's dining room filled far outweighed the headaches, she reminded herself. Besides, at the moment dealing with a temperamental chef was the least of her worries. Her real worry was Jackson Hawke. Just the thought of him made the pounding in her head increase.

Laura stepped into the elevator and pressed the button for the executive floor. If only the *real* emergency that Jackson Hawke had dropped in her lap could be solved as easily. Of course, she could always hope that the man was wrong—that her mother hadn't pledged her hotel stock and that Hawke hadn't actually bought her note. Laura called up an image of him in her mind's eye. She thought about the way he'd trained those blue eyes on her, the confidence in his expression, the hard line of his jaw. She sighed. Sure, she could hope he was wrong, Laura told herself. But Jackson Hawke hadn't struck her as a man who was often wrong about anything.

Stepping out of the elevator, she headed down the corridor toward the block of offices. When she entered the reception area and discovered her assistant on the phone, she retrieved her messages and began to flip through them.

Penny placed her hand over the receiver and mouthed, "Everything okay?"

Laura nodded and motioned for Penny to join her when she was finished with the call. Once inside her own office, Laura snagged a bottle of water from the mini-fridge and walked over to her desk. She opened the side drawer and reached for the bottle of aspirin. After shaking out two tablets, she washed them down with water and then sat in her chair. But five minutes later, Laura could feel the aura starting around the edges of her eyes and she knew the aspirin wasn't going to cut it this time. She was going to need the pills her doctor had prescribed for the migraines. She hated taking the meds, she admitted. While they knocked out her migraine, they also zapped her energy and made her feel fuzzy for the rest of the day. And today of all days, she needed a clear head and all the energy she could muster.

Shifting her gaze to the credenza, Laura glanced at the framed photo of her with her various half siblings and step-siblings at her mother's most recent wedding. She looked at the smiling green-eyed blonde beside her—her half sister, Chloe. At twenty-two, Chloe was four years her junior and the product of her mother's fourth marriage to soap opera star Jeffrey Baxter. An actress living on the West Coast, her sister was into healthy eating and treating the body's ailments with alternatives other than drugs.

Deciding it was worth a shot to try one of Chloe's methods before resorting to the pills, Laura began the deep-breathing techniques that her sister had shown her. And because she couldn't bring herself to chant the mantra aloud without feeling like an idiot, she repeated the words silently.

I can feel my heartbeat slowing. I can feel the blood flowing down my arms, to my fingertips. My fingers are growing warmer. I can feel the tension leaving my body. I am relaxed. I am calm.

Continuing the silent chant, she closed her eyes. But the minute she did so, an image of Jackson Hawke filled her mind. She remembered in vivid detail the cut of the charcoal-gray suit he wore, how the blue in his tie was the exact shade of his eyes. Even seated, he had looked tall and forbidding as he'd told her that he now owned the Contessa. And just thinking of Hawke made her head pound even harder.

"So much for natural healing," she muttered and opened her eyes. Still reluctant to take anything stronger than aspirin, Laura lowered her gaze to the bottom drawer of her desk.

Don't do it.

Ignoring the voice in her head, Laura pulled open the drawer and stared at her stash of candy. She had banished the forbidden sweets from her sight two weeks ago in her effort to cut her sugar intake and take off the five pounds she'd been carrying on her hips since Halloween. Biting her lower lip, she recalled the promise she had made to herself only three days ago. No more junk food. That meant no cookies. No candy. No ice cream. No milk-chocolate bars with the gooey caramel inside.

Don't do it, Laura.

Torn, Laura stared at the tempting treats. Her mouth watered. Still she hesitated. She'd promised herself, no sweets unless it was an emergency. Didn't Jackson Hawke and a monster headache constitute an emergency? Of course they did, she reasoned. Snatching up the bite-sized chocolate-and-caramel bar, she ripped off the wrapper, bit into the decadent treat and moaned.

"Uh-oh."

Laura opened her eyes and spied Penny

standing in the doorway. She popped the remainder of the forbidden chocolate into her mouth and swallowed. Calories or not, she felt better already, Laura decided.

After taking a seat in the chair across from her desk, Penny glanced at the candy wrapper and said, "Since Chef André didn't walk out like he keeps threatening to do, I'm guessing that guy Hawke is the reason you deep-sixed the new diet. Who is he, Laura? And what did he want?"

Laura gave her assistant a quick rundown of the situation and the stunned look on the other woman's face mirrored her own feelings when Jackson Hawke had dropped the bombshell on her an hour earlier. But now that some of the shock had started to wear off, she knew she had to figure out a plan to stop Hawke. "I know this is a shock, Penny. It was to me, too. But I need you to keep quiet about this—at least until I can find out exactly what our position is. If word were to get out, it could cause a panic among the staff and I can't afford that. It's been difficult enough getting workers since Hurricane

Katrina," she said, referring to the storm that had nearly destroyed New Orleans in 2005. Not only had the city lost more than half of its population, but the destruction had claimed entire neighborhoods and depleted the workforce. "And any buzz in the marketplace about management changes could set off a run of cancellations, not to mention that we'd probably lose out on any contracts."

"I won't breathe a word," Penny assured her. She paused, worry clouding her brown eyes. "But what if what this guy Hawke says is true? What if he really does own the hotel? Do I need to start looking for another job?"

"Hawke didn't strike me as a stupid man. Regardless of what happens, he'll need someone who knows about the day-to-day operations of the hotel, where and who to go to for the emergencies that pop up. And that person is you. I don't think you need to worry about your job, Penny."

But her assistant's concern made her realize that if Hawke did take over the hotel, Laura would need to do everything she could to ensure the job security of her employees. It was what her grandfather would have done, what he would have wanted her to do. If only her grandfather were here now, she thought.

"What about you? If Hawke is telling the truth, what will you do?"

"I don't know," Laura told her honestly. She thought about her childhood, of moving to new places each time her mother married and started a new life. But come summer, she had always returned to New Orleans, to her grandfather, to the Contessa. Even when she'd gone away to college and then had gone to work for other hotels out of state, she had known that the Contessa was still there, waiting for the day when she would return home for good. Only now when she had finally come back, her grandfather was gone. And Jackson Hawke was here, trying to take the Contessa from her. She wouldn't let him.

She couldn't. She looked at her assistant. "But I can tell you what I'm not going to do and that's roll over and play dead. Try Benton's office again, then get my attorney, my mother and my sister on the phone for me."

If Jackson Hawke wanted her hotel, then he was darn well going to have to fight her for it.

Two

So far, she'd struck out. Sighing, Laura put down her pen and stretched her arms above her head. She still hadn't spoken with her attorney or her sister. And her conversation with Benton had not gone well at all. She still couldn't believe her mother had actually used the Contessa as collateral on a loan and not told her. Benton hadn't given her much in the way of details. Instead he'd referred her to her mother. Unfortunately, the time difference and distance between New Orleans and France had made reaching her mother difficult. Glancing at the clock, she calculated the time overseas and concluded it was now after two o'clock in the morning in France. Aware of her mother's love of the night life, Laura tried the number again.

"Oui," her mother answered on the fourth ring, her voice breathless.

"Mother, it's Laura."

"Laurie, darling," she replied, genuine pleasure in her voice. "Philippe, it's Laurie calling from America."

She could hear Philippe shout out a greeting from the background and Laura made the obligatory hello to her mother to give to him. "Mother? Mother?" Laura pressed when her mother began to converse with Philippe in French.

"I'm sorry, darling. Philippe wanted me to tell you how well things are going here with the new club and to see when you can come for a visit. He's eager to show it off to you and Chloe." Without waiting for her to answer, her mother went on, "Do you think you girls could come? Why, it's been nearly a year since I've seen you,

Laurie. And it would be so lovely to have my babies here for a visit. We could…"

Laura closed her eyes a moment as her mother rambled. She didn't bother trying to explain to her that at twenty-six and twenty-two, she and Chloe could hardly be considered babies. Finally, she said, "Mother, please. This is important. I need to know if you used your stock in the Contessa as collateral for a bank loan."

For a long moment, her mother was silent. Then she said, "It was just as a formality. A guarantee, until I paid back the loan."

Telling herself not to panic, that not even her mother could have spent all that money so quickly, she asked, "How much of the money do you have left?"

At her mother's silence, the knot that had formed in her stomach when Jackson Hawke had walked into her office tightened. Just when she thought her mother wasn't going to respond, she said, "I don't have any of it left."

Laura felt as though the wind had been knocked out of her. There was nothing left? All of the money was gone? Suddenly a roaring started in her ears. Her stomach pitched. Feeling as though she were going to be sick, Laura leaned forward and put her head between her knees.

"Laurie? Laurie, are you still there?"

When the initial wave of nausea had passed, Laura straightened and leaned back in the chair. Lifting the phone receiver she still held in her hand to her ear, she managed to say, "I'm here."

"Darling, you sound…strange. Are you okay?"

No, she wasn't okay, Laura wanted to scream. Her foolish, reckless mother had placed the Contessa at risk. And because she had, Jackson Hawke might very well be able to take the hotel away from them, away from her. "You're sure it's all gone? There's nothing left?"

"I'm sure."

"What did you do with all that money?" Laura demanded.

Her mother explained how she had invested six million dollars into the nightclub that Philippe had been so keen to open in France. "I used some of it to pay for repairs to the hotel that the insurance didn't cover after the hurricane and the rest of it went to pay the back taxes on the hotel."

Laura knew the hotel had been underinsured at the time of the hurricane and, as a result, not all of the repairs had been fully covered. But the taxes? "The taxes couldn't possibly have been that much," Laura argued. "Since the hurricane, the assessment values have decreased, not increased."

"The taxes were from before the hurricane… from when your grandfather was still alive and running the hotel."

Laura frowned. That didn't make any sense, she thought and told her mother so. "Granddad always paid the Contessa's bills—even if it meant using his own money to do it. He would have made sure the taxes were paid."

"Apparently, he didn't. Or he couldn't. Evidently, the hotel wasn't doing well for quite some time before your grandfather became ill and he got behind on some of the bills. The tax assessor came to see me not long after the funeral and told me the taxes were three years in arrears, plus there were penalties. He was going to put a lien on the hotel. So I went to the bank and borrowed the money to pay them off."

Once again, Laura felt as though she'd had the wind kicked out of her. She'd known the hotel had gone through a rough patch and that her grandfather had hired a marketing firm to help him. But she hadn't realized things had been that bad. "Why didn't Granddad tell me? I would have come home and helped him with the hotel."

"That's probably why he didn't tell you, because he knew you would have come rushing home. And that wouldn't have been good for your career."

But Laura suspected her grandfather hadn't told her because he hadn't believed she was capable of running the Contessa. A sharp sting went through her as she recalled her grandfather dismissing the idea of her working at the Contessa after she'd graduated from college. He'd insisted she was too green to run a property like the Contessa and had told her to take the job she'd been offered by Stratton Hotels. Lost in thought, Laura didn't realize her mother had spoken until she heard her name said sharply. "I'm sorry. What did you say?"

"I said, how did you find out I pledged my stock to the bank for the loan?"

"Because the bank sold your note, Mother."

"Yes, I know. To some company with a bird's name."

"Hawke Industries," Laura supplied and she certainly didn't consider the man for whom the company was named to be some tame, feathered creature. Rather he was a predator—just like his name implied.

"That's right. I remember getting a notice from them, telling me they owned the note for my loan now."

"They own more than the note, Mother. You defaulted on the loan and now Jackson Hawke owns eighty percent of the stock in the Contessa."

Jackson Hawke sat in the penthouse suite of the Contessa Hotel late that evening and waited for the e-mail on Laura Spencer to arrive on his computer. Following his meeting with her, he had had the investigative firm he used compile a complete background check on her. He'd asked for everything—from her favorite flavor of ice cream right down to her shoe size. He frowned as he recalled his assistant's remark that it sounded personal. It wasn't, Jack told himself. It was business. Strictly business. And he intended to keep it that way.

As he waited for the file, Jack took a sip of his wine and considered, once again, his earlier encounter with Laura Spencer. While he had anticipated her objections and could even understand her denial at losing the hotel, he hadn't expected to find her outright defiance so stimulating. If he were honest, Jack admitted, the woman intrigued him. And it had been a very long time since anything or anyone had truly intrigued him.

A beep indicated the new e-mail and Jack clicked onto the file document and began reading the investigator's preliminary report. Much of the information he was familiar with already, having attained the data during his initial investigation of the Contessa and its principals. But he skimmed through the basics on Laura Spencer again anyway—noting the names of her parents, the schools she had attended, the places she had lived, her employment history. As he perused the information in the file, he paused at the newspaper and magazine clippings Fitzpatrick Investigations had included with the report.

He studied a color photo that had appeared in a soap-opera magazine more than twenty years ago of a young Laura on the steps of a church following her mother's wedding to an actor. Another photo showed a six-year-old Laura standing with her grandfather in front of the Contessa Hotel as the older man shook hands with the city's mayor. Even then, there was no mistaking the stubborn tilt of Laura's chin, the pride in her eyes, the promise of quiet beauty in her features. More clippings followed. Laura graduating as valedictorian from a high school in Boston. Laura in her freshman year at college in New Orleans. Laura making her society debut as a maid in one carnival ball and reigning as queen in another. Laura named as an assistant manager at the Stratton West Hotel in California. He paused at a more recent clipping of an elegantly dressed and smiling Laura on the arm of a man wearing a tuxedo. Jack clenched his jaw as he recognized her escort—Matt Peterson. Just the sight of his stepbrother's face sent anger coursing through him. And along with the anger came the painful memories, the old hurt. Jack read the caption beneath the picture.

Ms. Laura Spencer and Mr. Matthew Peterson at the Literacy Gala hosted by Mr. and Mrs. Edward Peterson.

How had he missed this? And just how serious was Laura's relationship with Peterson? he wondered. After dashing off an e-mail to Fitzpatrick Investigations, demanding answers, he considered how Peterson's involvement with Laura might impact his deal. While his stepbrother didn't have the money to bail Laura out, Peterson's old man and stepmother did. And there was nothing the pair wouldn't do for their golden-boy son.

Bitterness rose like bile in his throat as Jack thought of Peterson's stepmother—his own mother—who had left her family for her husband's business partner and best friend. Whether Laura was seriously involved with Matthew Peterson didn't matter, Jack told himself. All that mattered was the deal. If his stepbrother tried to play knight in shining armor for Laura, it would only make the deal that much sweeter when Jack foreclosed on the hotel and crushed Matthew in the process.

Irritated, but not sure why, Jack shut off his computer. Deciding he needed to stretch his legs and clear his head, he pocketed his room key and exited the hotel suite.

Twenty-five minutes later, he returned to the hotel, carrying a paper bag filled with a large cup of coffee and a chocolate éclair that he'd picked up at a hole-in-the-wall coffee shop located a few blocks from the hotel. While the crisp November air had refreshed him and tempered his restlessness, it had also awakened his appetite. One foot inside the tiny shop and he'd opted for the sugar-laden pastry.

"Evening, Mr. Hawke. I see you found the place I told you about," the doorman remarked as he approached the hotel.

"I sure did, Alphonse. Bernice said for you to come by and have a slice of apple pie and a cup of coffee after your shift," Jack said, relaying the message the waitress had asked him to pass on to her sweetheart.

Alphonse grinned, showing a mouthful of even white teeth. "That little girl makes the finest apple pie in all of New Orleans," he boasted. "You be sure to try some before you head home."

"I'll do that," Jack promised as he entered the hotel, his gaze sweeping over the lobby. He noted the magnificent chandelier, the marble floors, the artwork and massive urn of fresh flowers that spoke volumes about the hotel's quality. As nice and lucrative as the newer chain hotels were, they couldn't duplicate the old-world elegance and sense of history found in a place like the Contessa.

Despite the toll time and the lack of funds had taken on the hotel, the Contessa still exuded an air of luxury and privilege to those who walked through her doors. It was on the promise of that luxury and privilege appealing to the discriminating traveler, as well as the movie community that had adopted the city, that he had banked fifteen million dollars. It was a good investment, one based on numbers, not sentiment, Jack told himself as he pressed the button for the elevator.

After pushing the button again, he waited for one of the hotel's two elevators to arrive. Two minutes turned into three, then four. When he hit the button a third time, he took another look at the large dial above the elevator banks that indicated the cars' positions. He noted that one of the elevators remained on the eighth floor while the other was making a very slow descent from the twelfth floor. When it, too, stopped at the eighth floor, he frowned. Walking over to the front desk, he read the clerk's name tag and said, "Charlene, I think there's a problem with the elevators. They seem to be stuck on the eighth floor."

"I'm sorry for the inconvenience, sir. We've been having a little trouble with the elevators lately. I'll notify maintenance right away and have them check it out. I'm sure they will be operational in a moment," she advised him and picked up the phone to report the problem.

Making a mental note to add servicing and refurbishing the elevators to his list of immediate hotel improvements needed, Jack headed for the stairs. When he reached the sixth floor where the executive offices were, he paused before opening the door. He told himself he was simply going to check the status of the elevators and find out if they were moving again. But when he reached the elevator bank, he angled his gaze down the hall toward the management offices, where the lights were still burning.

A check of his watch told him it was after ten o'clock—long past quitting time, even for the hotel's general manager. But as he approached the suite of offices, he didn't have to wonder who'd be working so late.

Jack looked to his left toward Laura's office.

The door was slightly ajar and he could hear music—a hauntingly beautiful piece that was one of his own favorites. Obviously, he and Laura shared similar tastes in music.

Pausing in the doorway, he saw that Laura was seated behind the mahogany desk, her head tipped back against the massive black leather chair and her eyes closed. He used the moment to study her. The hair that he had classified as a color somewhere between red and brown that morning was a deep, rich red in the lamplight. Her skin was fair and had a smooth, creamy glow. Jack could just make out the faint dusting of freckles across Laura's nose. His gaze dipped to her mouth. Her lips were bare—no splash of bright color, no slick of gloss—which made her far more attractive in his book. She'd shed the red suit jacket she'd worn earlier to reveal a long, smooth neck and more creamy skin. The white silk blouse gently skimmed her shoulders and draped breasts that were neither large nor small, but just the right size to fill a man's hands.

As though sensing his presence, she opened her eyes. For the space of a heartbeat, she didn't move. She simply stared at him. Then suddenly she straightened and reached for the stereo remote. The music died midnote.

"You didn't have to turn it off. That CD is a favorite of mine," he told her and stepped into the room.

Ignoring his comment, Laura's voice was cool as she said, "If you're looking for your room, Mr. Hawke, it's on the top floor."

"Thank you for pointing that out, Ms. Spencer," he said. So she had discovered he was a guest in her hotel. He'd known that she would. A good general manager made a point of reviewing the hotel's guest list. She had apparently reviewed hers and found his name on it, which, judging from her expression, had not pleased her. He walked over to her desk and set down the bag with his coffee and éclair.

"The business office is closed."

"And yet you're still here," he pointed out. "I didn't realize being the hotel GM meant working day *and* night. I'm surprised your boyfriend doesn't object to the long hours."

"Was there something you wanted, Mr. Hawke?"

He paused a moment, considered the loaded question and the woman. Evidently from the way she narrowed her eyes, Laura realized what he was considering had nothing to do with business. Deciding it was best not to go there, he finally said, "Actually, I was taking the stairs up to my room when—"

"Why were you using the stairs?"

"Because the elevators aren't working."

When she grabbed for the phone, he reached across the desk and caught her wrist. Gently removing the telephone receiver from her hand, he replaced it on the cradle. "The front desk has already alerted maintenance."

Laura pulled her wrist free. "I'm sorry you were inconvenienced," she told him. "I'm sure maintenance will have the problem fixed shortly. In the meantime, if you need to get to your room, you can use the service elevator. I'll show you where it is."

"That's okay. I'm in no hurry. I'll just wait for the elevator," Jack told her. Deciding to take advantage of the fact that he had her one-on-one, he sat down in the chair in front of her desk. "But since I'm here and you don't appear to have any pressing meetings scheduled at the moment, maybe now would be a good time for us to talk about the hotel. I'm assuming you've spoken with the bank and confirmed my ownership position of the hotel."

"Actually, I haven't confirmed anything other than the fact that you purchased my mother's note. And until I speak with my attorney and find out what your legal claim is on the property, I see no reason for us to have any discussion about the hotel."

"All right. We won't discuss the hotel. But I would like to drink my coffee before it gets cold. That is, if you don't mind," he added even as he removed the large foam cup from the paper bag. He took out the chocolate éclair that was wrapped in a thin white pastry sheet. Looking over at her, he noted that her eyes were trained on the treat. "Maybe you'd like to join me? I bought the large-size coffee."

"No, thank you," she said.

"Some of the éclair, then?"

"No, thanks," she told him, but Jack didn't miss the way she looked at the pastry.

Ignoring her protest, he divided the éclair in two and placed half of the chocolate pudding-filled confection on one of the napkins, then set it in front of her. When she simply stared at it, he said, "Go ahead."

"I'm not hungry," she told him.

"What's hunger have to do with it?" he asked and bit into his half. He didn't bother to hide his enjoyment. The rich pudding inside the choco-late-iced pastry shell was delicious. "Alphonse was right. Bernice does make the best éclairs."

"This came from Bernice's Kitchen?"

He nodded, took another bite, swallowed. "I was looking for a cup of coffee and wasn't exactly dressed for the dining room," he said, indicating the casual slacks, sweater and bomber jacket he wore. "Alphonse recommend Bernice's."

"Bernice is a genius when it comes to baking." The wariness in her expression faded, giving way to a look of anticipation as she dragged her fingertip through the chocolate pudding spilling from the torn pastry. "I tried to hire her as a pastry chef for the Contessa, but she turned me down flat. Said she didn't think it was a good idea for her and Alphonse to be working at the same place, that it might take some of the mystery out of their relationship."

Jack arched his brow. "I got the impression they were in a…um…long-term relationship."

"They've been dating for fifteen years, engaged for the last four. They don't want to rush things," she told him, the hint of a smile curving her lips.

"After fifteen years, I'd say there's little chance of that happening."

"It seems to work for them," she said and brought her finger to her mouth.

There was something inherently sensual about the sight of Laura licking her finger, Jack thought. He found himself wondering what she would look like while making love. Would those green eyes darken with need and heat? Would her lips part, her breathing quicken? Would that smooth, cool skin feel as soft as it looked?

The direction of his thoughts annoyed him, but it didn't surprise him, he admitted. He was a healthy male who enjoyed the opposite sex and the pleasures to be found in a woman's body. But when it came to women and sex, he had no delusions. Plain and simple, he believed in lust, not love. And right now he was experiencing a serious case of lust for Laura Spencer.

She scooped another finger full of pudding and as though sensing his gaze, Laura looked up. Her body went still. Her eyes locked with his as awareness sizzled like electrical currents between them.

Jack watched as Laura's lips parted and when he heard the slight hitch in her breath, he felt another stab of lust. The pudding on her fingertip fell with a splat onto the napkin on her desk. But her eyes remained locked with his. Not bothering to think about what he was doing or how it might impact his business, Jack pushed back his chair and started toward her. He had just reached the side of her desk when he heard the tap at the door.

A disapproving male voice came from the doorway asking, "Am I interrupting something?"

Three

For a moment, Laura couldn't breathe. The air seemed to have backed up in her lungs as Jackson Hawke stood at the side of her desk looking at her as though he wanted to swallow her whole. And heaven help her, for a moment, she had almost wanted him to.

"Laura?"

Shaking off the moment of insanity that had gripped her, Laura yanked her attention to the doorway where her attorney, Daniel Duquette, stood looking both concerned and curious. "Daniel," she said, her voice sounding more breathless than she would have liked. She cleared her throat. "What are you doing here?"

Daniel strode from the doorway into the office, slanted a glance at Hawke before shifting his focus back to her. "I've been tied up in depositions in Baton Rouge all day and just got back. When I picked up my messages, there was one saying that you needed to see me, that it was urgent. The front desk said you were still here, so I decided to stop by on my way home. Is everything okay?"

Everything was far from okay, Laura thought. But now was not the time to go into all that was wrong—not with Jackson Hawke standing there, measuring Daniel with his eyes and on the heels of whatever madness had stricken her. Because it certainly had been sheer madness that had caused her to react to Hawke as she had. The man was her enemy, she reminded herself. "Not exactly. And I do need to talk with you," she said, hoping Hawke would take the hint.

"I think that's supposed to be my cue to leave," Hawke said drily before he shifted his gaze from her to Daniel. "I don't believe we've met. I'm Jackson Hawke," he said and extended his hand.

Daniel shook his hand. "Daniel Duquette," he replied, his brow creasing. "You wouldn't happen to be the same Jackson Hawke with Hawke Industries who engineered the takeover of the Wilhelm family's company last year, would you?"

"Guilty as charged."

As she witnessed the exchange, Laura had a vague recollection of the small chain of family-owned inns that had been bought out by a corporation. She'd heard that the sale hadn't been a friendly one, that the two brothers who'd owned the properties that had been in their family for years had been split on whether or not to sell. There had been a great rift in the family because of it and because of the sale. The man behind that had been Jackson Hawke?

"So what brings you to New Orleans, Mr. Hawke?"

"Business."

"Thanks for sharing the éclair," Laura said,

eager to get rid of Hawke and talk to Daniel about the mess her mother had gotten them into.

Hawke held her gaze for several moments. "You're quite welcome."

"Good night, Mr. Hawke."

He dipped his head in acknowledgment, but Laura didn't miss the gleam in his blue eyes that told her he hadn't forgotten what had almost happened between them. "I'll call your assistant in the morning about scheduling that meeting. Duquette," he said with a passing glance, and without waiting for a reply he strode out of the room.

The door had barely closed when Daniel asked, "What was that all about? And what's Jackson Hawke doing here?"

Laura sat down in her chair and released a breath she hadn't even realized she'd been holding. "He's the reason I called you. My mother pledged her stock in the Contessa as collateral for a bank loan and defaulted on the loan. Hawke bought her note and now he's trying to take over the Contessa."

Daniel let out a whistle. "Damn."

"My sentiments exactly," she said. "I spoke with the bank chairman briefly by phone and he wasn't much help. I'm going to meet with him after the Thanksgiving holidays. I know it's late, but could you take a look at these documents and tell me if there's anything I can do to stop Hawke from taking over the hotel?"

"Sure. Let's see what you've got." Daniel removed a pair of glasses from his coat pocket, slipped them on and began to read through the sheaf of papers she'd handed him. "I assume your mother received notices from both the bank and Hawke telling her she was in default of the loan," he said as he flipped through the pages.

"She remembers receiving something about the payments being late. She meant to contact them and explain she needed an extension, but because of the time difference and the new club opening, she never got around to making the call." Laura cringed inwardly as she heard herself repeating her mother's excuse. It was typical Deirdre behavior, she thought. When confronted with a problem, more often than not, her mother would go into her Scarlett O'Hara mode and plan on dealing with the matter another day. Only she never did deal with the problem. It either took care of itself or it got worse. But this time her mother's irresponsibility had proven disastrous.

Finally, he removed his glasses and looked up. "It looks legit. Unless your mother can come up with fifteen million dollars in the next thirty days to repay the loan, Hawke Industries can claim the stock she pledged as collateral and take over the hotel. I'm sorry, Laura."

So was she. But she refused to give up and play dead. Already, a plan was forming in her mind. "In other words, if I can come up with the fifteen million dollars and pay off the loan before the thirty days are up, then Hawke can't take the hotel. Right?"

"Right. But where are you going to get fifteen million dollars?"

"I don't know," she told him honestly. "But I'm not going to just hand over the Contessa to Jackson Hawke without at least trying to save her."

* * *

He had given her enough time, Jack decided. It hadn't been easy, but he had made himself wait three days—until after Thanksgiving had passed. Since his mother had walked out on him and his father all those years ago, holidays had been just like any other day as far as he'd been concerned. On those few occasions when his father had attempted to make Thanksgiving or Christmas some warm, fuzzy family event, it had invariably ended with Samuel Hawke pining for the woman who'd run out on them both, then drowning his heartache in a bottle of whiskey. Once his father had died, Jack had been able to stop pretending that holidays were some special family affair.

But something told him that that was just what they were for Laura Spencer—special, warm and fuzzy family affairs. He couldn't help wondering how she had spent her Thanksgiving. He knew her mother was in France and that her father lived on the East Coast. He also knew she had a slew of step and half siblings scattered across the country. Evidently, she hadn't traveled to see any of them since she was already at the hotel on the Friday morning following the big turkey day.

Or had she canceled her plans because of him? It was a strong possibility that she had, he conceded. Pushing aside a twinge of guilt that he might have caused her to spend Thanksgiving alone, Jack assured himself that Laura would make up for it at Christmas. She'd probably fly to France and spend it with her mother, he reasoned. Unless, of course, she was planning to spend Christmas with his stepbrother, Matt.

Jack considered that a moment, recalled one of the few times he had visited his mother, her new husband and stepson. The visit had been at Christmas and the entire scene had been something out of a Norman Rockwell painting—only it was a picture in which Jack hadn't belonged. Laura would belong though. He frowned at the image of Laura with Matt and his family gathered around a Christmas tree, opening gifts, drinking eggnog. According to Fitzpatrick Investigations, she and his stepbrother had been seeing each other for more than a year and it was rumored they'd been seriously involved when she had moved back to New Orleans.

Jack frowned. He knew Matt Peterson. The man thought far too highly of himself to restrict himself to any one female. A leopard didn't change its spots and neither would his stepbrother. Laura might think that she was the only woman in Peterson's life, but Jack would bet his vintage Corvette that there were several someone elses. But if Peterson had devoted a year to Laura as the report indicated, his stepbrother had done so for a reason. More than likely that reason had something to do with the senatorial race Peterson was rumored to be considering. Jack considered that angle for a moment. Laura was pretty, smart, well educated and poised. While her parents might be maritally challenged, her family tree was a good one and Laura herself was scandal-free. She would definitely be an asset on a senatorial candidate's arm and help him to get votes. Her return to New

Orleans would have put a kink in Peterson's plans, but Jack doubted the man had abandoned his goal. He might have shelved it for a while, but Peterson didn't like losing any more than Jack did. It had been one of the few things they'd had in common. According to Fitzpatrick's report, the pair had supposedly remained "close" friends despite her move. Just how close were they? he wondered. How many times had Matt tasted her mouth, touched that soft-looking skin, felt her body beneath his?

Envy sliced through him like a scalpel, swift and sharp. Annoyed by the stab of jealousy, Jack reminded himself that his stepbrother had nothing that he wanted. All Jack wanted was to get down to business. Determined to do just that, he entered the executive offices of the hotel. "Is she in?" he asked the receptionist, his voice sharper than he'd intended.

"Yes, but—"

Ignoring her attempts to waylay him, he marched into Laura's office. "Good morning," he said as he approached her desk.

"It was."

Dismissing the barb, Jack met her gaze. Her eyes were the same clear green as the waters in St. Thomas, he decided, and damned but he couldn't help wondering what it would take to make those eyes turn dark and smoky for him. Irritated with himself and her, Jack decided there was no point in dancing around his reason for being there. His voice was cold, brusque, as he said, "I assume you've had an opportunity to speak with your attorney by now."

"I have."

He put down his briefcase and withdrew the management contract he had prepared for Laura, along with the purchase agreement for her stock. He also pulled out the letter of resignation he'd had drawn up in the event it was needed. While the transition would be simpler for him if she stayed on at the hotel, he was prepared for her to quit and to buy out her stock. "Then you know that my purchase of your mother's note is legal."

"Legal, maybe. But certainly not ethical."

Refusing to debate her, he continued, "Then you also know that by defaulting on the loan, she forfeited the stock that she pledged as collateral on the loan. Which means Hawke Industries now owns the controlling interest in the Contessa."

He paused, waited for her to respond. But Laura remained silent. Her demeanor remained unchanged.

Keeping his voice level, he said, "My plan is to turn the Contessa into a five-star property again and recapture the market share it's lost. As I've already told you, I would prefer that you stay on at the hotel as the general manager. But if you choose not to stay, then I'm prepared to accept your resignation and purchase your stock." He slid both agreements and the resignation letter across the desk so that they rested in front of her. "It's your call, Ms. Spencer. Are you going to stay? Or are you leaving?"

Laura didn't even look at the documents he had placed before her. Instead, she met his gaze. There was something hard and determined in her eyes as she said, "I'm not going anywhere, Mr. Hawke."

The news surprised him. After their previous conversations, he had been sure she would turn him down flat. The fact that she hadn't both pleased and concerned him. He was pleased because it would be good for business to have her stay on. It concerned him because he had the hots for her, he admitted. And she was more than likely sleeping with his stepbrother, he reminded himself. The thought of Laura with the golden boy his mother had chosen as her son over him chafed at Jack, made him feel raw. He couldn't help wondering how Peterson would feel to come out on the losing end for once. Irritated with himself for allowing his thoughts to stray from the business at hand, he tapped the documents on the desk. "In that case, I'll need you to sign a new management contract with Hawke Industries. It's pretty straightforward, with all the standard clauses and the increase in salary I mentioned earlier."

"I'm sure the contract is fine."

He nodded. "Still, you may want to have your attorney look it over anyway."

"That won't be necessary."

"It's your call," he told her.

"Yes, it is."

Jack wasn't sure why, but her agreeable demeanor seemed off. "There's also a purchase agreement for your stock, if you should change your mind about selling it. My previous offer of—"

"I won't change my mind."

Something was off, Jack told himself again. Instinct, some unexplained ability that told him if a venture would be a hit or a flop, kicked in now. The woman was up to something. He felt it in his gut, felt it in his bones. "Why do I get the feeling that you're just itching to throw those contracts in my face?"

She picked up the contracts, fingered them. Looking directly at him, she smiled and said, "Because I am."

There was a confidence in her smile, a spark in her green eyes that he found intriguing. Intriguing and sexy as hell. "I admire your honesty. But you might want to think twice before you do that."

"Why? Because it would be an unwise career move on my part?" she asked.

"Something like that."

"You'd probably be right—if you were my boss and had the authority to fire me," she began. Obviously too edgy to sit, she stood and paced behind her desk. She paused, turned and looked at him. "But you don't."

"The last time I checked, owning eighty percent of the stock in a company constitutes the controlling interest, which does make me your boss and gives me the authority to pretty much do whatever I damn well please."

"That would be true—if you owned the stock. But you don't own it. At least not yet," she informed him triumphantly.

"Is that so?"

"Yes, that's so. You see, that note that you so cleverly got the bank to sell you gives me thirty days to cure the default on my mother's loan.

Once I do that, my mother keeps her stock in the Contessa and your deal, Mr. Hawke, is null and void."

So that was her plan. Jack would have laughed were it not for the fact that this stunt of hers would cost him both time and money with delays. He didn't intend to allow her to cost him either—not without a price. "You think you can go out and find fifteen million dollars like that?" he asked with a snap of his fingers.

"I didn't say it would be easy."

"Try next to impossible."

"Nothing's impossible," she fired back at him.

"Trying to block my purchase of this hotel is," he assured her. Standing, he walked around to her side of the desk, a deliberate move on his part to intimidate her. Instead he found himself far too aware of her, of the way the office light caught the copper in her hair, the way her black silk blouse curved over her breasts, the way the scent she wore reminded him of exotic islands and sex. Desire hit him like a one-two punch. He wanted her. Maybe part of him wanted her because she belonged to his stepbrother. But another part of him wanted her because he sensed a fire in her and he wanted to be the one to ignite it.

"Why? Because you're so rich and powerful?"

"Yes." Leaning closer, he lowered his voice and said, "And because I never lose."

"There's a first time for everything."

Jack didn't bother to hide his amusement. "And you think that you'll be the one to beat me?"

"I don't think I can beat you, Hawke. I *know* I can."

"You sound pretty sure of yourself."

"I am," she insisted.

Before he could quell the impulse, he countered, "Sure enough to wager on the outcome?"

"You mean a bet?"

"That's right. You say you can stop me from taking over the hotel. I say you can't. Are you willing to put your money where your mouth is?"

"I am, if you are," she told him.

"Oh, I am. I most definitely am."

* * *

She was insane to have dared the man the way she had, Laura admitted. But blast him, he had been so smug, so sure of himself. The fact that he had been standing so close to her hadn't helped, either. She had hoped those moments of heightened awareness between them in her office a few nights ago had been a fluke, that stress and thoughts of spending the Thanksgiving holiday without any of her family had caused her sexual chemistry radar to go askew. But if it had, then her radar still wasn't working because she'd felt those same ripples of awareness when he'd entered the room, that same quickening of her pulse each time he drew closer.

"So what are the stakes?"

"The stakes?" she repeated, doing her best to shake off his effect on her nervous system.

"Yes. You know, the prize that you're going to fork over to me when you lose our bet and I foreclose on the Contessa."

Laura sobered at his cocky remark. Taking a step back, she said, "You mean the prize that *you're* going to fork over to me when I beat you at your own game."

His lips twitched. "So what are the stakes?"

"Dinner," she suggested. "The loser pays for a seven-course meal at the restaurant of the winner's choice."

"Dinner?" he scoffed. "That's your idea of a bet?"

"What do you expect me to offer? My car? My condo?" she tossed back at him, and suddenly felt queasy at the thought of losing either.

"I don't have any use for a three-year-old BMW and you don't have enough equity in your condo to make it worth my trouble."

Anger bulldozed right over any misgivings she'd had about challenging the man as she realized he had had her investigated. Temper driving her, she put her hands on her hips and looked him square in the eyes. "And just what are you going to give up when you lose and *I* win?"

"I have a Jaguar that you'd look good in," he

said with a smile that lit up his eyes and made his face go from handsome to dangerously sexy.

"Far be it from me to take away your little toy and force you to be driven around in a limo."

"And I'd hate to have to see you hoof it to work in those high heels or be forced to sleep on the couch in your office," he countered.

He didn't think she could do it, Laura realized. He honestly didn't believe she could outmaneuver him and save the hotel. She could see it in those blue eyes, sense it in the way his muscles had tightened when she'd challenged him. She could feel it in the way he was watching her now—like a hawk with a helpless mouse in his sights. The realization that he thought she'd already lost only fed her temper. And it was her temper that had the words falling off her tongue as she declared, "Believe me, I won't be the one hoofing it to work or sleeping on a couch, Hawke."

"You won't have to. After all, it really wouldn't be fair of me to foreclose on your hotel, then take your car and home, too."

Suspecting that he was trying to bait her, Laura

kept a rein on her temper, determined not to let it get her into any more hot water. With a nonchalance she was far from feeling, she said, "Well, since you ruled out dinner, I guess the bet's off."

"Not necessarily," he said.

"We can't agree on the stakes," she pointed out.

He stared at her for a long moment, long enough for Laura to see his enjoyment in sparring with her turn to something else, something hot, something sexual. "I have another idea on what the stakes could be," he said finally. "But I've got a feeling you're not going to like it."

Laura knew at once what those stakes were. She'd seen it in his eyes the very first time he had looked at her, felt it the other night when he had almost kissed her. He wanted to have sex with her. That he would even suggest such a thing infuriated her. It also made her stomach tighten, her skin heat. "You're right. I don't like it. And despite what you might think, going to bed with you just isn't my idea of a prize."

He laughed. "That's a pretty big assumption you've made."

Laura could feel the color rush to her cheeks and cursed her fair skin. Refusing to back down, she said, "All right. So what *did* you have in mind?"

"Never mind my idea," he said, his amusement fading. He inched a step closer. That dark and hungry look was back in his eyes, in his voice, as he said, "While it's not what I had in mind initially, I like your idea better. A lot better."

"The bet was a stupid idea in the first place. Let's just forget the whole thing," she told him, hating the fact that just having him move closer made her heart start racing again.

"Why? Don't think you can pull it off after all?"

Pride had her spine stiffening and the words firing from her lips. "I know I can pull it off."

"Then the bet stands. When I win, you spend the night in my bed."

Laura's pulse scattered. "And what do I get when I win?" she demanded, wishing she had never started this thing, wishing she could figure a way to get out of it without losing face…or something more.

"Your mother's promissory note—free and clear—and you get to keep or return the money you borrowed."

Laura blinked. "You can't be serious. That would mean you'd lose the fifteen million dollars you paid for the note."

"I won't lose," he assured her.

His words set her competitive juices stirring once again. She so wanted to wipe that smug look off his face. "Like I said, there's a first time for everything."

He grinned. "If you're right, then you have nothing to worry about. But if you're wrong and you can't come up with the money in time, then I foreclose on the hotel and I get you—in my bed for an entire night."

It was crazy. No, it was beyond crazy, she thought. It was insane. *He* was insane. Because only a madman would make such a bet. "Not that I'm complaining, mind you. But don't you think the stakes are a bit lopsided? At least for you. I mean, it hardly seems fair that I stand to have a fifteen-million-dollar loan wiped out whereas all you stand to gain is a night of sex."

He ran his eyes down the length of her in a way that made her skin feel as though he had touched her. "I'm satisfied with the stakes."

"I should think a man with your ego could satisfy his sexual needs for a lot less money," she tossed back, annoyed by her reaction to him.

"Oh, but I'd much prefer to have those needs satisfied by *you,* Ms. Spencer," he said, his voice dropping to a seductive whisper that sent a shiver along her nerve endings. "So, do we have a deal?"

For a moment, Laura said nothing. She was every bit as crazy as he was to even consider such an outrageous thing, she reasoned. The man was a corporate shark. Every article and interview she had been able to dig up on him all proclaimed his genius as a businessman. He hadn't lied. He seldom lost. When it came to doing business—or in the Contessa's case, engineering a hostile takeover—Jackson Hawke would be a lethal opponent. And regardless of how good she was at her job, she'd be lying to herself if she thought that finding the money she needed to cure the defaulted loan would be easy. At best it was a long shot. But if she could pull it off, somehow raise enough money in time, she would win the bet, get the Contessa and be able to pay back the loans. "You're really serious? You'd risk fifteen million dollars against a night…a night of sex?"

"A night of sex with *you*," he amended. "And, yes, I'd risk it."

Still, she hesitated. She'd be a fool not to accept the deal he was offering her. And if she lost?

"Of course, if you're ready to concede that you can't come up with the money and dispense with the thirty days so I can foreclose, we can call off the bet."

Laura yanked up her chin. "I'll do no such thing. You've got yourself a bet. And if I were you, Hawke, I'd get ready to lose fifteen million dollars."

He smiled, a knowing smile that made the air

in her lungs grow shallow. "And if I were you, Spencer, I'd get ready to spend a night in my bed—without the benefit of sleep."

Four

Jack stood on the corner outside the restaurant where he'd gone for dinner and waited for the light to change. Still restless despite the long walk, he hit the speed dial for Fitzpatrick Investigations. When it went to voice mail, he grimaced. "It's Hawke. I need you to get me whatever you can find on Matthew Peterson, both personal and business. And I need it ASAP. Send whatever you find to my e-mail address."

Hitting the off button, he considered calling his assistant at home, then opted against it. Unless it was an emergency, Dotty would not be at all happy to have him calling her at home on a Sunday night. As she'd told him often enough, weekends were for family.

Instead, he holstered his cell phone and when the light changed, he headed back down Saint Charles Avenue in the direction of the hotel. The air was cool, but not cold like New York. Not that you could tell by the way the people were dressed with their gloves and heavy coats, he thought. And given the number of red-and-green scarves he'd seen, people were already into the Christmas frenzy. December was still a few days away, but the storefronts and restaurants were already trimmed in lights. Christmas trees filled several windows and wreaths hung from doors. Even the lobby of the Contessa sported pots of red and white poinsettias and a huge tree.

Jack frowned as he thought of how all the Christmas craziness was going to impact him getting business done. He hated the distraction the holidays caused almost as much as he hated weekends. And he really hated weekends, Jack admitted. Nobody wanted to work on weekends and unless you were in the retail or service end of business, nobody did. That meant there were no stock deals to be done, no bank transactions to be made, no business brokering to negotiate and no attorneys or board of directors available to draw up contracts and vote on his deals. He hated that. He hated wasting time and he hated waiting for the hours to tick by until Monday morning rolled around and he could get back to work.

Sidestepping a couple with a baby stroller, Jack continued toward the hotel. Despite what his assistant claimed, he was not a workaholic who needed a wife. He had all the female company he wanted. As for work, it was mastering the game that drove him. That and the need to win. And having Laura in his bed was a bet he was looking forward to winning. He was thinking about all the delectable ways he intended to enjoy Laura when he neared the hotel and spied her standing under the porte cochere with her back to him and a cell phone at her ear. As he drew closer, he caught the tail end of her conversation.

"No. It's just that I was hoping we could go tonight to see the Celebration in the Oaks together."

He knew from the doorman that the Celebration in the Oaks was some big Christmas thing at the park. Was she talking to Peterson? he wondered. Was he in town? Was Peterson the reason he hadn't seen Laura at the hotel all weekend? Jack clenched his jaw as he thought about Laura spending the past two days with his stepbrother. He had never liked Matt Peterson. Even when their fathers had been partners and friends, the two of them had never gotten along. Two years older than him, Peterson had been a manipulative bully who had gotten his kicks by getting Jack into trouble. Later, when his mother had run off with Peterson's father, Matt had delighted in taunting him, calling him and his father losers.

"Yes. Of course I understand. Business should come first."

For a moment, Jack heard his mother's voice in his head, admonishing him for eavesdropping when he'd overheard her making plans to meet his father's partner. He didn't care if it was wrong or rude, he decided, and dismissed the memory. He remained where he was, several feet away from Laura, but close enough to listen to what she was saying. Although he made a show of studying the firs that had been draped with white lights near the hotel's entrance, his focus remained on Laura and her conversation.

"I know. It's just that it's been a while since I've seen you and I was looking forward to us spending some time together."

The disappointment in her voice had envy curling in his gut. The fact that he was fairly sure it was his stepbrother she was pining over made the uncharacteristic jealousy he was experiencing all the more difficult to swallow. It also made him angry—with her and with himself—and all the more determined to wipe every memory of Peterson from her mind when he claimed her as his prize. The admission sent a stab of guilt through him. Just as quickly, he dismissed it. He was not using Laura to exact revenge on Peterson, he told himself. The chemistry had been there between them even before he'd known she was involved with his stepbrother. The fact that he would be taking her from Peterson when he bedded her would simply be an unexpected bonus.

"No. Don't worry about picking me up. I'm just going to take a taxi home and call it an early night." She paused. "You, too."

After she flipped the phone closed, she turned around and stopped cold when she saw him. "Hawke, what are you doing out here?"

"I was on my way into the hotel when I thought I recognized you standing over here. I wasn't sure it was actually you at first since this is the first time I've seen you in jeans—which, by the way, look great on you," he added. It was the truth. Those long legs of hers were made for skirts, but they looked every bit as sexy in the snug-fitting jeans.

"Thanks."

"You're welcome." Judging by her body language, Jack could see that he was making her nervous and he wasn't sure if that pleased him or not. He wanted her nervous with anticipation about being in his bed, not nervous because she was afraid of him. "I haven't seen you around the hotel the past couple of days and was beginning to think you were avoiding me."

"I decided to take the weekend off and catch up on some personal stuff."

Personal stuff like hooking up with his stepbrother? he wondered and felt that envy burning his gut again. "Have you told your boyfriend about our little bet yet?"

"I haven't told *anyone* about our bet," she informed him.

"Why not? Afraid he won't like the idea of you sleeping with me?"

"*I* don't like the idea that there's even the remote possibility that I might have to sleep with you. So I'd just as soon no one else know that I agreed to something so stupid."

Irritated by her response and his need to prove her a liar, Jack inched a step closer. He wanted to haul her up against him, kiss her senseless until she was begging him to make love to her.

And because his own need was so great and he feared he wouldn't stop with a kiss, he did neither. Instead, he reached out and drew the back of his fingers gently down her cheek. His gaze never left her face and he watched her eyes widen, darken at his touch. Then slowly, very slowly, he rubbed his thumb along her bottom lip. Her lips parted. He heard her gasp, felt the warmth of her breath against his fingertips. He was reconsidering kissing her after all when Laura stepped back.

"I need to go," she said and started to leave.

"Laura, wait," he called as he followed her toward the hotel's entrance.

He wasn't sure if it was because he'd called her by her name or if she heard the regret in his voice, but she stopped, turned. Before he could apologize for coming on like a Neanderthal, she held up her hand and said, "No, you wait. I don't know if you're trying to intimidate me or seduce me, but it isn't going to work because I'm not going to sleep with you. At least, not unless I have to."

"Fair enough."

"I—" Evidently surprised by his answer, she fell silent, leaving the rest of what she'd planned to say unfinished. "Then I guess there's nothing more to say except good-night. So if you'll excuse me, I think I'll go grab a taxi and head for home."

"What about the Celebration in the Oaks?" Jack asked as he fell into step beside her. When she slanted a glance his way, he explained, "I couldn't help overhearing. Sounded like your boyfriend canceled on you."

He waited for her to confirm or deny his statement. She did neither. Not until they stopped at the end of the line for the taxi stand did she say, "Something came up. I'll just go another time."

The disappointment in her voice was also in her expression. And, once again, Jack found himself irritated by the notion of her with Peterson. A burning need to wipe his stepbrother's memory from her mind and replace it with his spread through him. "Alphonse said this Celebration in the Oaks is some kind of Christmas-lights display in the park. He said that it's worth seeing."

"It is," she assured him as a gust of wind blew down the street. Pulling up the collar of her denim jacket, she brushed the hair away from her eyes. "The gates open at dark every night from now until the end of the year. You should go see it while you're here."

"You still here, Ms. Spencer?" Alphonse said as she reached the front of the taxi line. "Evening, Mr. Hawke."

"Alphonse," Jack said.

"I thought you were over at City Park looking at the pretty Christmas lights with your—"

"Something came up and we had to cancel," she told him. "But I'm going to need a taxi to get home."

"No problem," he said and whistled for the next cab to come forward. "Sorry you didn't get to go see the Oaks, ma'am. I know how much you loved going to see them with your grandfather."

"Thanks, Alphonse. But I'll just go see them another time."

The taxi arrived and Alphonse opened the door. But before Laura got in, Jack caught her arm and said, "Why wait? Why not go now? With me."

Laura still wasn't sure what had possessed her to agree to accompany Jack to view the Celebration in the Oaks. Granted, her moods had been all over the place for nearly a week now—ever since Jackson Hawke had walked into her office and pulled the rug from beneath her high heels. Her emotions had run the gamut—from anger to despair and fear, from hatred to outrage and lust—and every one of those emotions had been ignited by Hawke. But of all of them, it was her attraction to the man that worried her the most. When she'd found herself wanting him to kiss her, she'd realized just how dangerously close she'd come to making a monumental mistake.

The man was her enemy, she reminded herself. He was a thief out to steal her legacy. And whether she won or lost the foolhardy bet they'd made, she'd be an idiot to risk losing her heart to the man. Yet, when he'd asked her to come with him to the Celebration in the Oaks, there had been something in his eyes, a loneliness, that had touched something deep inside her. She'd remembered the staff telling her that he'd ordered room service and spent Thanksgiving Day alone in his room. It made her realize how fortunate she'd been because she'd never spent any holiday alone. It was one of the advantages, she supposed, of her parents' multiple marriages. There was always family somewhere and she was always welcome. Last year had been one of the few times she hadn't celebrated Thanksgiving with her own family, opting instead to join Matt and his family.

She thought of Matt, realized she hadn't called him back as she had promised. And while she had used her sister, Chloe's, visit as an excuse for cutting the conversation short, the truth was she hadn't wanted to go another round with Matt. While she cared deeply for him, she didn't love him—at least it wasn't the kind of love that her grandparents had shared, the kind of love that she wanted. And despite his claim, she didn't believe that Matt really loved her that way, either. If he did, he would have understood why the Contessa meant so much to her. He didn't. Nor did he understand why she'd left California and returned home to try to salvage the hotel. He certainly wouldn't understand her desperation now to save it from falling into the hands of Jackson Hawke.

Shifting her glance, she took advantage of the dimly lit backseat and studied Hawke. In the jeans and bomber jacket, he seemed far less forbidding, she thought. With his black hair mussed from the wind and the beginnings of a five-o'clock shadow darkening his jaw, he was, surprisingly, even more handsome. But even dressed casually, there was an air of alertness, a fearlessness and determination that exuded power. There was also something inherently sensual about him that told her this was a man of passion, a man of strong appetites. The fact that he'd made it clear he wanted to indulge those appetites with her should have appalled her. And it did. But it also ignited a longing inside her that had desire curling in her belly whenever she was near him.

Embarrassed by the admission, Laura stared out of the taxi window and warned herself what a mistake it would be if she were ever to let Hawke know just how tempting she found him. Her silent warning was still ringing in her head when the taxi swerved to avoid a pothole and sent her body careening sideways, nearly into Hawke's lap. Pressing her hands against his chest to right herself, Laura looked up and made the mistake of glancing into his eyes. The heat simmering in them set off a tingling sensation inside her. Suddenly aware that his arms were cradling her, she straightened and scooted back to her side of the seat. "Sorry," she murmured.

"No problem," he told her, the husky timbre in his voice only adding to the charged atmosphere.

"Sorry about the rough ride, folks," the driver said, his eyes meeting theirs in the rearview mirror. "These here streets took a real beating in

Katrina, and being under water for all those weeks didn't help."

"We understand," Hawke told him, but his gaze remained fixed on her.

"The streets weren't in the best of shape even before the storm and now they're a whole lot worse," she commented, trying to diffuse the moment. As though to prove her point, the car hit another rut that had her body bumping against his again. He made no comment as she returned to her side of the taxi and this time, she held on to the hand grip above the door.

"She's right," the taxi driver commented, apparently oblivious to the tension. "A lot of the streets are still a mess. But the people are starting to come back. And mark my words, New Orleans is gonna be just fine. It's just gonna take more time than most folks thought."

While the driver answered a call from his dispatcher, Jack said, "He's right about it taking longer for the city to recover. I imagine leaving a hotel like the Stratton West to take over operation of the Contessa wasn't an easy decision."

"It was for me," she said, grateful that he was focused on business and not on her.

"Really? Most people in your position wouldn't have given up a big paycheck with a growing operation so easily."

"I'm not most people," she informed him.

"No, you're not. Maybe that's why you intrigue me, Laura Spencer."

Unsure how to respond, Laura chose to remain silent and spent the final minutes of the drive looking out the window, trying to ignore the man seated beside her. Eager to escape the intimacy of the darkened car, she was already unbuckling her seat belt as the taxi pulled up to the entrance of the park.

"This is as far as I can take you, folks," the driver informed them as he parked the car. "No driving tours allowed anymore, not since Katrina."

After paying the taxi driver, Jack joined her in line.

"Since you paid for the taxi, I'll take care of the entry fees."

But before she could even open her wallet, he

handed the admission clerk a crisp fifty-dollar bill. "I've got it," he said. "You can buy us coffee later."

Too eager to see the display to argue with him, Laura said nothing. Once they had their hands stamped, they walked into the park and she entered a virtual wonderland of lights. She tried to take in everything at once—the towering oak trees dripping with white lights that looked like stars, the Christmas trees and storybook characters fashioned from lights, the delight on the faces of the children as they spied Santa Claus.

"Is it like you remembered it?"

Laura glanced to her side and realized Jack was watching her. "Yes. And no. A lot of it's the same, but it's different, too. There used to be more trees, more lights," she explained as the two of them began to walk through the park. "There was a road over there where cars could drive through and see all the lights. On the really cold or rainy nights, that's what a lot of people did. There were also horse-drawn carriages you could take the tour in. When Chloe and I were younger, we used to sing 'Jingle Bells' and pretend we were riding in a one-horse open sleigh."

"A sleigh, huh?"

She didn't have to look at him. She could hear the smile in his voice. Laughing, she shrugged. "What can I say? We're snow-deprived Southerners."

He laughed.

The sound surprised her. It was the first time she'd actually heard him laugh. Unable to resist, she sneaked a peek up at him. He was smiling, and not just that slight twitch at the corners of his mouth, but an honest-to-goodness smile that revealed perfect teeth and radiated in his eyes. For the first time since she'd met him, Jackson Hawke actually looked happy, she thought. And she wasn't sure why, but knowing that she was responsible made her feel warm inside.

"Is that a train I hear?" he asked.

"Yes," Laura told him, suddenly enjoying herself. "There's a miniature train ride that goes through the park and there's this huge elevated train exhibit that has these tiny replicas of the streetcars and historic buildings and landmarks around New Orleans. It's like a mini-version of the city. Come on, I'll show it to you."

Laura showed him the train exhibit. She showed him Storyland. She showed him the vintage rides in the Carousel Gardens, sadly pointing out that several were no longer working because of the damage they'd sustained in the storm. She showed him the gallery of Christmas trees decorated with handmade ornaments made by local schoolchildren that lined the walkways of the Carousel Gardens. Finally, she showed him her favorite part of the exhibit—the antique wooden carousel. "It's more than a hundred years old," she told him and explained how the severity of the storm and the exposure to water had left the carousel inoperable. "I know it doesn't look all that great now because the paint is faded and chipped and so much of the gilding still needs to be redone, but you should have seen it before the storm. It was beautiful."

"I'm sure it was. It's amazing it even survived the storm."

"It's a miracle. I just hope they'll be able to get the funds they need to restore it. Since the park doesn't get any state or federal funding, the only money for repairs has to come from donations and admissions. With the population half of what it was pre-Katrina, there's less money." She sighed. "It would be such a shame if other little girls and boys never got to ride on it like I did."

"Boys, don't run," a harried-looking and very pregnant woman called out to the twin boys wearing green jackets and matching hats who were streaking toward them. "Please, would you catch them for me?"

"Whoa," Jack said, reaching out and corralling them. "Hey, buddies, what do you say we wait for your mom?"

"You're big," one of the boys said. "Are you a Saints football player?" he asked, referring to the city's beloved team.

"Afraid not. But you guys are so fast, I bet you could play for them when you get big."

"I'm so sorry," the woman said as she reached them. She smoothed a hand over her stomach.

"Their little sister makes keeping up with them harder than it used to be."

"Not a problem," Jack told her. "We were just chatting about football. I think you've got yourself two running backs in the making here."

The woman laughed and ruffled their heads. "Their daddy would love that. In fact, he's home watching Sunday-night football right now. I must have been out of my mind to not make him come with me."

"We're going to see *The Cajun Night Before Christmas* exhibit," one of the boys said.

"Are you now?" Jack replied.

Both boys nodded. "It's supposed to be just like the book. If you want to see it, you just need to follow this road."

"Over there?" he asked, pointing in the direction they'd indicated.

"Yeah."

Still hunkered down beside the boys, Jack lowered his voice and said, "You know, I could have sworn I saw one of Santa's elves hiding up in one of those trees over there."

Both boys' eyes grew wide as they looked toward the trees. "Really?"

Jack nodded. "I figure they must be here, checking out the boys and girls and reporting to Santa which ones are extra good. You boys might want to walk with your mom so they can tell Santa how good you two are."

"Come on, Mom. You'd better hold our hands and take it slow."

"Yeah, you shouldn't run. You might trip or something," the other twin added.

"Thanks," the woman mouthed as she and her sons headed in the direction of the trees with the elves.

"That was really sweet of you. I'm sure their mother was very grateful," Laura told him, touched by his actions.

"Hey, I was telling the truth. I think I did see an elf in those trees," he said, smiling once again.

"Which tree?"

"That one right over there," he said and, grabbing her by the hand, he brought her several yards back from the road and pointed up to a huge oak. "That one. I saw a pair of little green eyes peeking out of those branches."

Laura peered up at the branches in question. "I don't see anything," she told him and when she turned to look at him, the smile dissolved on her lips. He was still holding her hand and he was watching her with an intensity, with a longing, that stole her breath.

She didn't know how it happened. She didn't know if he took another step toward her or if she moved toward him. Then his mouth was on hers. The kiss was gentle, slow, just a simple brushing of lips against lips. Then she felt the tip of his tongue. Sighing, she opened her mouth to him. Heat exploded inside her and just when her senses hit overload, he was easing back, ending the kiss. Still dazed and wondering why he had stopped, she heard the voices. A family was approaching on the path near them.

"I didn't think you would want an audience," he said simply.

He was right. She wouldn't and it embarrassed

her that she had been so engrossed in the kiss that she hadn't heard them. "Thanks."

"Don't thank me. For a moment there, I considered not stopping," he told her as he brushed his thumb along her jaw.

Confused and shaken by his effect on her, Laura stepped back and in doing so pulled her hand free. She walked back over to the carousel to take another look at it before leaving.

Jack followed and stopped beside her. "So tell me about the carousel."

"What do you want to know?"

"About the history of it. How long it's been here. How old you were the first time you came to see it."

Laura filled him in on the history, or as much of it as she knew. She told him how it had been her grandfather who had first brought her to see it. "I was four at the time," she told him. "My mom was married to Jeffrey Baxter, the soap star, then, and we were living in California. She had just had Chloe and was finding a four-year-old and a newborn a lot to handle. So she sent me down here to visit my grandfather. I was feeling a little homesick, so he took me to see the Christmas lights in the oaks to distract me. And the minute I saw the carousel, I fell in love with it."

"Which one was your horse?" he asked.

Laura looked over at him, surprised at his perceptiveness. "The palomino over there, with the red saddle," she said, pointing out the horse she had always ridden. "I named him Pegasus."

"The flying horse, huh?" he remarked because it was one of the horses crafted with its legs in flight.

"Yes," she said and laughed at herself. "I really did think he could fly. In fact, I had myself convinced that the carousel was enchanted and that when everyone left for the night all the horses and animals would come to life."

"Ever test your theory?"

"Yes," she admitted proudly and smiled at the memory. "When I was six, I snuck away from my grandfather just before closing time and went and hid in the carousel house."

"What happened?"

"None of the carousel animals came to life, but everyone else did. My grandfather and the security guards and staff were looking for me. My grandfather thought I'd been kidnapped and everyone was upset. I got in a lot of trouble with my granddad and wasn't allowed to have any desserts or treats for an entire week after that."

He let out a whistle. "No desserts for a week? That must have been really tough," he said, but from the grin on his face, it was clear he didn't think it had been tough at all.

"Trust me, it was torture," she assured him with a laugh. "I'd have sooner given up my favorite doll than give up dessert for a week."

"Have a sweet tooth, do you?" he teased.

"I was six," she pointed out. Then recalling how his appearance had caused her to hit her candy stash, she amended her answer by saying, "I've gotten better." But the memory of *why* she'd hit the candy stash in the first place brought reality crashing back. The man she had been sharing such tender moments with was Jackson Hawke. Her enemy. The man who was trying to foreclose on her hotel. The man with whom she'd made the crazy bet and agreed to sleep with if she lost. "It's getting late. I'd better see about getting a taxi and heading home."

"What about the rest of the exhibit?" he asked.

"I think we've seen everything."

"What about that new one—that Cajun story one."

"*The Cajun Night Before Christmas.* It's an animated children's story by a local author and artist. I wouldn't have thought you'd be interested," she said honestly. In fact, she wouldn't have thought he'd be interested in any of the exhibits, but he'd seemed to genuinely enjoy himself. And if she were honest, she had enjoyed sharing them with him.

"I wouldn't have thought I'd be interested, either, but I am."

The man confused her. He was a mass of contradictions. Just when she had him pegged as a rich and arrogant man who would wager a fifteen-million-dollar note against a night with her in his bed, he spendt an evening looking at Christmas lights with her and listening to stories about her childhood. On the one hand, she despised the businessman who threatened to take away a part of her heritage. On the other hand, she liked the kind man who had been so gentle with the little boys and considerate of their mother. She liked the man who had laughed with her, the man who had made her first visit to the carousel since her grandfather's death a happy one.

"Laura?"

The sound of him calling her by her first name snapped her out of her reverie. "Yes?"

"You zoned out there for a minute. Either that or I shocked you into silence. Which is it?"

"Both," she admitted.

"So what do you say? Do you want to see that other exhibit with me?"

Laura hesitated. Spending more time with this man wasn't a good idea, she told herself. She was beginning to like him, feel drawn to him. The last thing she could afford was to lose her focus when the Contessa was at stake. "I think I'll pass. But you go on ahead."

"Maybe another time, then," he said. "I'll head back to the hotel."

But when the taxi arrived, Jack insisted on sharing it with her. He also insisted the driver take her home first. Once they reached her place and she'd tucked her share of the cab fare into his hand, she said, "Good night."

He touched her arm. "Laura?"

She paused, turned to face him. "Yes?"

"Thanks for tonight. I'll see you in the morning."

And in the morning, he would be her enemy again, she reminded herself as she quickly exited the taxi and raced up the steps to her house.

Five

Seated in the dining room of the Contessa Hotel, Jack kept his eyes trained on the doorway and awaited the arrival of Chloe Baxter. Fitzpatrick had managed to locate Laura's half sister—in New Orleans, where she had been since Thanksgiving weekend. Funny how Laura had failed to mention the fact that her sister was visiting. But then, she had studiously avoided him since that night they'd gone to see the Christmas lights in the park. On those occasions when their paths had crossed, she had been all business. It was as though the woman he had laughed with and kissed in the park had never even existed.

Only he hadn't been able to stop thinking about that woman. It was difficult for him to look at her and not remember how sweet she had tasted, how good she had felt in his arms. Even more difficult was wondering if his stepbrother was the personal business she'd left town for two days ago. Jack closed his fist around the glass of Scotch as he considered that possibility. According to the detective, there had been no record of Peterson booking a flight in or out of New Orleans last weekend. But knowing Peterson's tastes and ability to manipulate, he could just as easily have gotten someone to fly him in on a private plane. Maybe one of his rich college buddies or someone in the moneyed crowd his father was so tight with. Or maybe even one of the corporate idiots that Peterson had conned into backing his political run.

Or maybe he'd been wrong and Peterson had never been in town after all. Had Laura gone to see him? It certainly would explain her sudden

leave on personal business. According to Fitzpatrick Investigations, she had booked a flight to
San Francisco with a stop in L.A., and there
were no hotel reservations anywhere in her
name. But then, why would she need a hotel
room if she was sleeping with his stepbrother?

A white-hot anger seethed inside him at the
image of Laura with Peterson. He tossed back a
swallow of Scotch, but it did nothing to soothe
the gnawing in his gut. If she was with his stepbrother, it wouldn't be for much longer, he
assured himself. He knew through his sources in
the financial arena that her attempt to secure a
personal loan from the bank by pledging her
own stock as collateral had been turned down.
With only twenty days left on the thirty-day
proviso, she was running out of options quickly.
Once the designated time to cure the default was
up, the hotel—or at least eighty percent of its
stock and the controlling interest in it—would
belong to him.

And so would Laura.

He would win their bet. And once he had her in

his bed, he would wipe any trace of his stepbrother from her body, from her mind, from her soul.

Jack frowned. He was competitive. No one did what he did for a living without possessing a strong competitive streak. The truth was he enjoyed a challenge, thrived on taking risks. The higher the stakes, the more exciting he found the game. And he'd be lying to himself if the thought of taking Laura from Peterson didn't appeal to him on a very personal level. It did.

But it was more than that, Jack admitted. Even before he'd known about her connection to his stepbrother, she had set his competitive juices flowing and his hormones into a state of lust. Just remembering how she'd looked that night in the Carousel Gardens with her cheeks flushed, her eyes filled with desire and her body taut sent adrenaline pumping through his system. She'd been like some wild creature and every male hormone in his body demanded that he capture and possess her.

Disturbed by the admission, Jack shoved the images from his mind. Laura had been right.

Making that bet with her had been crazy. *He* had been crazy. To offer the note he'd paid fifteen million dollars for against a night with her in his bed had been insane. It didn't matter that she stood little chance of winning the bet. The fact that he had even agreed to the terms had been flat-out reckless. Worse, it had been the act of a man making a decision guided by his hormones instead of by sound business sense.

So why did you do it, Hawke?

Because he wanted her. And he fully intended to have her.

"Would you like another Scotch, Mr. Hawke?"

Jack glanced down at his empty glass, then up at the waitress who stood at his table. Dressed in a crisp black-and-white uniform and wearing a name tag with Tina written on it, she gave him a friendly smile. Reasoning that he had no farther to travel than the elevator to his room, he said, "Sure."

"I'll be right back," she told him and wove her way through the busy restaurant toward the kitchen.

Shaking off his disturbing thoughts about

Laura, Jack glanced around the restaurant. There was a nice crowd, he noted. Laura's decision to open the dining room on weeknights to draw from the local business clientele leaving work had been a smart move. So had extending the dinner hours on the weekends. Both were moves he would have implemented himself. Some well-placed advertisements and a few local TV and radio spots to capitalize on the popular chef's affiliation with the Contessa would fill the remaining tables. He made a mental note to discuss a series of print and TV ads with Laura. Of course, that was assuming she agreed to stay on as general manager when she lost the bet.

The bet.

Had Laura been thinking about those stakes as much as he had? he wondered. That kiss they had shared had given him a glimpse of what it would be like between them. Even now he wondered how the night might have ended had he not played the gentleman and ended it when he had.

"Here you go," the waitress said as she placed the Scotch in front of him.

"Thanks." Jack started to take a sip, then decided against it. Instead, he picked up the knife on the place setting before him. Made of quality stainless steel, he noted as he traced the blade with his fingertip. It was also sharp enough to cut his finger if he wasn't careful. A lot like Laura, he thought—attractive, of excellent quality and dangerous if a man wasn't careful.

He was always careful, Jack reminded himself. Putting aside the knife, he checked his watch. Thirty minutes late. Evidently, punctuality wasn't one of Chloe Baxter's virtues, he decided. He was just beginning to wonder if the woman would be a no-show when he spied the striking blonde in the doorway. At first, he wouldn't have pegged her for Laura's sister. On second glance though, he noted the shape of her eyes and the long legs were very much like Laura's. She was a real head-turner, Jack thought as the hostess led her toward his table. Judging by the number of appreciative male looks cast her way, he wasn't the only one who thought so. He stood as she approached. "Ms. Baxter," he said and extended his hand. "I'm Jackson Hawke."

She shook his hand firmly. "Mr. Hawke," she said in a voice that had a smoky tone to it.

Once she was seated, he asked, "Would you care for something to drink?"

She looked up at the waitress, smiled. "I'd love a glass of merlot."

Jack ordered a bottle from a select vintage and once the waitress was gone, he said, "I appreciate your agreeing to meet with me."

Amusement lit her hazel eyes. "We both know that I came here in exchange for your promise that you'd schedule a meeting with Meredith Grant to discuss her company, Connections."

"Yes. And I have to say, your request surprised me. As an actress, I would have thought you would have traded for an introduction for yourself to a producer or casting director. After all, I do know several. But instead, you asked for something for a former stepsister. Why is that?"

"Meredith's my sister. Just because our parents divorced doesn't mean she and I stop being sisters. And contrary to what most people think, not all actresses are self-centered divas. Meredith has been trying for months to get an appointment with you and your office keeps turning her down." She sat back in her seat, crossed her legs and met his gaze. "When you called and asked me to meet with you, I saw an opportunity to get her that appointment and took it."

Jack nodded. "I appreciate your candor, Ms. Baxter."

"Then I hope you'll appreciate that I intend to have you book that meeting with Meredith before I leave here today."

"I'll book the meeting—just as long as both you and Ms. Grant understand that I'm not interested in a matchmaking service."

"Connections does more than matchmaking," she told him. "It connects people for business reasons, too. That's what Meredith wants to meet with you about."

"Very well, Ms. Baxter. I'll keep my promise and book the meeting with Ms. Grant," he assured her. "In exchange, you promised to listen to my offer and hear about my plans for the hotel with an open mind. Agreed?"

"Agreed," she replied. "And the name's Chloe."

"Very well, Chloe. And my name's Jack."

"All right, Jack. I'm listening."

She listened while he told her about his reasons for wanting to buy the hotel. She listened as he explained the difficulties of competing in the hotel market in the post-Katrina city. She listened as he told her about his plans to restore the Contessa and make it a viable, revenue-producing property.

"If you're able to do what you say, it seems the smart thing for me to do would be to hold on to my stock because it'll be worth a lot more down the road."

"That's true. But that's at least a year or two away," he said as he leaned back in his chair. "Accepting my two million dollars now would mean you wouldn't have to take another waitress job and you could study full-time at the L.A. Theater Institute."

She lifted her eyebrow. "I suppose I shouldn't be surprised you did your homework on me. Laura said you were smart."

"Did she now? What else did your sister say about me?"

She smiled. "I think she mentioned something about your being an arrogant Neanderthal who—"

Laughing, he held up his hand. "I think I get the picture."

"I thought you would," she said with a twinkle in her eye. "Although I'm not sure the Neanderthal fits. I expected you to be bigger…and ugly."

He laughed.

So did she.

And they were both laughing when an unsmiling Laura walked into the dining room. Damn, but she looked good, Jack thought. No suit today, he noted. She was dressed in an ivory sweater with a red ribbon bow shooting across the shoulder and a skinny-fitting skirt of lipstick-red that gave him an enticing view of those killer legs. Her mouth was painted that same shade of red and Jack found himself itching to taste it.

"See something you like, Jack?"

Jack shot a look over at Chloe and, given the

amused expression on her face and tone in her voice, his appraisal of her sister hadn't gone unnoticed. As Laura approached their table, Jack stood. "How was your…vacation? It was a vacation, wasn't it? Your assistant said you were off on personal business."

"My trip was fine," Laura said drily, her attention focused on her younger sister. "Hello, Chloe."

"Hi, sis. You're back early. I thought your flight wasn't due in until after nine tonight," Chloe said.

"I was able to get an earlier flight. I thought you had a date tonight," Laura said, accusation in her voice.

"I do—but not until later. So I decided to take Jack up on his dinner offer."

He knew very little about siblings, particularly siblings who loved one another. His only experience had been the hurtful experiences and bitterness that permeated his relationship with Matt Peterson. Whatever was going on between Laura and Chloe was different—and whatever it was, it was generating a lot of tension. In an effort to diffuse some of that tension, he said, "We were just about to order coffee and dessert. Would you like to join us?"

"No, thanks. I've got some paperwork to catch up on. Besides, I wouldn't want to interrupt you while you're trying to charm my sister into selling you her stock."

Chloe waved her hand in dismissal. "Lighten up, Laura. As charming as he is, Jack already knows that I have no intention of selling him my stock. Don't you, Jack?"

He did know it. But judging by the look of relief on Laura's face, she hadn't been quite so sure. "Yes, I know you're not going to sell," he said. "But it doesn't mean I haven't enjoyed our time together or that I'll stop trying to convince you." He looked over at Laura. "Either of you."

"And as I've already told you, you're wasting your time," Laura said.

Annoyed by her dismissal and wondering whether or not a rendezvous with his step-brother, Matt, was the reason, Jack said, "Speaking of wasting time, before you take off on another trip, you might want to remember that there are only twenty days left before one of us has to pay up on that bet. I'm counting on that someone being you."

Back in her office, Laura tried to focus on the letters awaiting her signature and block out all thoughts of Jackson Hawke. The man was infuriating. She'd wanted to wipe that cocky smile off his face. And at the same time, she'd wanted to jump his bones. Just remembering the way he had looked at her—as if he'd wanted to swallow her whole—made her pulse stutter, her body hot.

"All right," Chloe said, marching into Laura's office and slamming the door behind her. "What's going on between you and Jack? And what's this about a bet?"

Laura didn't bother to look up from her paperwork. "I thought you had a date."

"Forget about my date. I want some answers."

Laura sighed. "Nothing's going on and the bet doesn't concern you."

"It sure didn't look like nothing to me. You two were generating enough heat between you to keep this hotel warm for the entire winter. And when Jack mentioned that bet, you turned as red as that skirt you're wearing before you stormed out of the dining room."

"You're wrong."

Chloe planted her hands on the desk, got in her face. "Laura, this is me you're talking to. I may not know anything about running a hotel, but I do know about sexual chemistry. And believe me, there was definitely some serious sexual chemistry cooking between you two."

Her sister was right, Laura admitted to herself. There was sexual chemistry between them. And for her there was something more, something she hadn't wanted. She had hoped that kiss in the park had just been a fluke, that these feelings she was starting to have for Jack weren't real and would disappear with the light of day and with some distance. But they hadn't disappeared. If anything, they were getting stronger. In fact, he was the reason she had come home early from California. She had actually missed him, had even wondered if she had misjudged him. She had gone so far as to hope that maybe she wasn't the only one who had felt there was something more than desire happening between them. Only when she'd seen him with Chloe, believing he was trying to buy her sister's stock, she'd realized she had been kidding herself. Sure, Jackson Hawke might want to have sex with her, but what he really wanted was the Contessa. His reminder that in twenty days he intended to take the Contessa from her only served to bring home that fact.

"Since I turned down two million dollars for my stock because this place means so much to you, I think I deserve some answers," Chloe pointed out. "Tell me what's going on and why you're so upset."

Laura told her sister everything. She told her about the bet she had made with Jack in the heat of the moment. She told her about the evening they had spent together at the park viewing the Christmas lights. She told her about the kiss and the feelings it had stirred inside her.

"It sounds to me like you might be falling for the guy," Chloe responded. "There's nothing wrong with that. You said you and Matt weren't exclusive anymore. And you can bet the wannabe-congressman isn't spending his nights alone. Or did he manage to convince you to change your mind about that when you were out in California?"

"Matt didn't convince me to change my mind about anything because I didn't see him. I went to see Papa Vincenzo and his family because I canceled on them at Thanksgiving," she said, referring to one of their former stepfathers.

"Then I don't see where you hooking up with Jack should be a problem."

"It's a problem because I'm not into one-night stands or casual sex. And that's what it would be with a man like Hawke."

"You don't know that," Chloe argued.

No, she didn't know it for a fact. But she had a pretty good idea that Hawke was not a man who was into long-term relationships or commitments. She was. "But I do know that the man's a shark. He's a corporate raider. Half the companies he buys, he dismantles and sells them off in pieces for a profit. And now he's intent on doing that to our hotel."

"Not according to him," her sister told her. "Besides, if you ask me, Mr. Jackson Hawke seemed a lot more interested in winning that bet and you than he is in foreclosing on the hotel."

"Yes, he is. Isn't he?" He did seem intent on the bet, Laura realized, and found herself wondering why. While she didn't doubt for a second that he wanted her, there had been moments when she'd caught him looking at her, with something more than desire in his eyes. There had been anger and determination and something else all mixed in with his wanting her. What she didn't understand was why. "Don't you find that odd? That he's more focused on the bet than the hotel?"

"What I think, dear sister, is you think too much." Walking around to the other side of Laura's desk, Chloe opened the drawer and stole a bag of chocolate-covered nuts from her stash. When Laura attempted to take them back, Chloe quickly moved out of her reach. "You know what else I think?" she asked as she ripped open the bag and popped several of the candies into her mouth.

"No. But I imagine you're going to tell me."

"I think Jackson Hawke's got a case of the hots for you. And I think you've got the hots for him. So I say quit analyzing it to death and enjoy it."

"And I say you're going to be late for your date," Laura said, wanting to end the discussion.

"All right, I'm going. But seriously, Laura, there are a lot worse things that could happen than to find yourself waking up in Hawke's bed."

There were a lot worse things that could happen than her ending up in Jackson Hawke's bed, Laura conceded. One worse thing that came to her mind was losing the Contessa Hotel. Not wanting to think about that possibility or about Jack, she fortified herself with a chocolate peanut-butter cup, then tackled the mountain of reports and correspondence that had accumulated in her absence.

After she'd finished going through the budget

reports and projections, she reached for the folder of incoming mail. A quick glance revealed several solicitations, bills and subscriptions. Then she spied an unopened envelope from the Jardine Law Firm. Her stomach pitched. It was the same firm that had handled the foreclosure paperwork for Hawke. Ripping open the envelope, she pulled out the document.

Quickly, she skimmed the legal jargon and zeroed in on the name *Hawke Industries*.

In accordance with Hawke Industries' purchase of the above-referenced note, Hawke Industries and/or its appointed representative are hereby granted access to said hotel property in order to perform the due diligence afforded Hawke Industries as purchaser of said note. Hawke Industries and/or its appointed representative will not be afforded the right to take any actions or implement any changes in the hotel, its management, personnel or operations until such time that the thirty-day grace period on the loan has expired and the shares of stock in the hotel are transferred to Hawke Industries. Also in accordance with the purchase of the above-referenced note, Hawke Industries and/or its appointed representative will be provided suitable office work space to perform said due-diligence process connected with the sale.

Laura didn't bother reading any further. He couldn't do this. He couldn't just waltz in and take over before the thirty days were up. And if he'd been planning to do this, why hadn't he told her? With temper blazing and the attorney's letter crumpled in her fist, she headed for the penthouse suite. The ride up the slow-moving elevator only added to her mood. By the time she exited the car, she was nearly trembling with anger and frustration. Marching over to the ornate door of the penthouse, she punched the doorbell to the suite. She counted to ten and when Jack didn't answer, she pounded on the door with her fist.

No answer.

She beat on the door again. "Hawke, open this door now." When he still failed to respond, Laura didn't hesitate. Reaching into her skirt pocket, she pulled out the master key card she always carried that allowed management access to all rooms in the hotel for emergency purposes. She zipped it into the lock. The green light kicked on, unlocking the door.

"Hawke, get out here," she demanded from the entrance.

Nothing.

"Hawke," she yelled as she tried to find him in the living and dining room areas. Ignoring the laptop computer and mounds of files, she began searching the rest of the suite. The first two bedrooms were empty. Growing angrier by the second, she pushed open the door to the master suite. Still no Hawke. She spied the door to the bathroom ajar, heard the buzz of an electric razor. Intent on confronting him, Laura made a beeline for the bathroom. She shoved the door open and sent it banging sharply against the wall.

And there Jack stood in front of the sink, naked from the waist up, with a towel anchored around his hips and a razor buzzing in his hand.

Surprise flickered across his features for a moment as he shut off the razor. "Hello, Laura. Was there something you wanted?" he asked, an edge in his voice.

At the sharp tone, Laura jerked her gaze from his bare chest to his face and remembered that she was the one with reason to be angry—not him. But before she could tell him so, he was moving toward her.

"Let me guess. Your trip didn't turn out quite the way you'd planned and your friend didn't come through with the money like you thought he would."

"What are you talking about?" she replied, confused.

But he didn't seem to hear her. "Isn't that why you're here, Laura? Because you know you can't beat me, so you've come to pay off on our bet?"

"In your dreams."

"Actually, I've had quite a few dreams about

having you in my bed, Laura. Especially after that night in the park. What about you? You have any dreams about what it'll be like between us?"

"*Nightmares* is more like it," she lied, vowing he'd never know that she had wondered what it would be like to make love with him. Even now she wasn't immune to him and was having a devil of a time ignoring the way the sprinkling of dark hair made a vee down his chest to his sexy abs before it disappeared beneath the towel hitched around his hips. Suddenly realizing what she was doing, Laura yanked her gaze back to his face. His mouth looked hard. His expression closed. But his eyes, his eyes were dark and hungry as they watched her watch him.

"If you're not here for sex, then why did you break into my room?"

"I didn't break in. I used the pass key," she informed him, holding up the card that she still held in her hand.

"Which is a violation of a guest's privacy and illegal."

"It's not illegal if you enter with cause," she defended, knowing that was a stretch.

He moved toward her, causing the towel to shift precariously. "And just what would that cause be, Laura?" he asked, his voice dangerously soft.

"This," she said, shoving the attorney's letter at him.

He barely gave the letter a glance. "How does notification that I'll be starting the due diligence on the hotel qualify as cause for illegal entry to my room?"

"Because I came to tell you that there isn't going to be any due diligence because there isn't going to be a foreclosure."

"Why? Did the friend you spent the past couple of days with lend you the money to stop me?"

"No. At least not yet." The truth was Papa Vincenzo hadn't given her an answer yet on lending her a portion of the money because he and his wife needed to meet with their accountants first. But even if they did give her a loan, it would only be for a fraction of the money she needed.

From the scowl on his face, her answer hadn't pleased him. "Pardon me," he said and she stepped to the side while he stretched out his left arm to the towel rack behind her. But instead of taking the towel and moving away, he continued to hold on to it, effectively caging her between him and the counter.

There was that look in his eyes again, that mingling of anger and desire, she noted. Laura's heart pounded as he leaned closer. Suddenly she was aware of how tall he was, just how wide those shoulders were. He smelled like soap and outdoors, she thought. Lifting her gaze, she stared at his face and noticed for the first time that his eyes were a blue so deep they were almost black. His hair was still damp and mussed from his shower, and she had this crazy urge to brush it away from his forehead. She noted the stubble along his chin that he hadn't had a chance to shave. She looked at his mouth, recalled how those lips had felt on hers that night in the park and all she could think was she wanted to kiss him again.

As though he could read her thoughts, Jack lowered his head until his mouth was only inches from hers. He waited a fraction of a second, no more. Yet it seemed like an eternity during which she could feel her pulse race, could feel her heart beat frantically like the wings of a hummingbird. And just when she thought surely she would explode, his mouth was on hers—hot, hungry, demanding. Somewhere Laura heard a moan. But she wasn't sure if it came from her or from Jack.

Then she couldn't think at all as Jack continued to kiss her. When she touched her tongue to his, Jack gentled the kiss. He kissed her slowly, deeply, thoroughly. Her head spun. Her stomach quivered. Every nerve in her body seemed to have come alive at the touch of his lips.

And she wanted more.

The papers she held in her hand fell to the floor, freeing her fingers to explore his face. She could feel the whiskers where she had interrupted his shave. She could smell the mixture of soap and a woodsy scent. She sieved her fingers through his damp hair and kissed him back.

One kiss strung into another and then another, each feeding that ache inside her, each one demanding more. Of their own volition, her hands slid down to his shoulders, to his chest, along the dusting of dark hair. When her fingers moved lower and unknotted the towel at his waist, Jack sucked in his breath. This time when she heard a groan, Laura knew it was Jack's. He devoured her with his mouth.

So caught up in the feel of him and the heat of his mouth, it took her a moment before she realized that Jack had stopped kissing her. When she opened her eyes and saw the hunger in his blue eyes, her heart began to race all over again.

"One of us is wearing too many clothes," he whispered in a voice that sent another wave of desire pumping through her. He drew the backs of his fingers slowly, gently, along the line of her breast.

Her nipples puckered. Her breath lodged in her throat and she closed her eyes, overwhelmed by the sensations. Even through her sweater and bra, she could feel the heat of his touch and another wave of desire pulsed through her. Opening her eyes, she looked at him, witnessed the strength of his arousal. The sight of him had heat pooling in her belly, between her thighs.

She took a step back and heard the papers crunch beneath her heel. Laura looked down, saw the letter from the attorney that had driven her to his suite in anger.

Suddenly sanity came crashing back. What was she doing? What had she been thinking? Hadn't she just told Chloe earlier that the man was a shark, that he was out to steal their hotel and score a one-night stand? She couldn't let him do either. Not and look at herself in the mirror in the morning. "This was a mistake. I never should have come here."

And without waiting for him to respond, Laura turned and ran from the bathroom and out of the suite.

Six

"**I** agreed to allow you to start the due diligence, didn't I?" Laura argued as she stood across the desk from Jack the next morning.

"Yes, you did. And I appreciate your cooperation," he told her, not bothering to point out that she really hadn't had much choice. She'd been on the defensive since his arrival that morning.

As he listened to her excuses for not providing him with the office he'd requested, he noted that she had taken great care to keep the subject on business. She'd made no mention of her visit to his suite the previous night or what had happened between them. He thought about that initial kiss, the anger that had driven him to possess her, the need to wipe Peterson from her mind and body until all she wanted was him. Only when she had kissed him back, she had tasted sweet and hot, just as she had that night in the park. Then all he could think about was quenching the thirst inside him with her. He had thought she'd felt the same way—until she had bolted from his suite.

Why had she bolted? It was a question he'd asked himself long after she had gone. And the answer he kept coming back to was Peterson. If she had been with his stepbrother as he suspected, Peterson wouldn't have told her about their connection since he'd never claimed Jack as part of his family. Instead he would have warned her to stay away from him, that he was ruthless, the son of a loser and not to be trusted. The last thing Laura would want would be for her lover to find out that she had slept with his sworn enemy. And Peterson would find out he'd bedded Laura, Jack vowed. He would make sure of it. Then he would see how his stepbrother felt to be the one who came out the loser. As for Laura, he wouldn't hurt her, he promised himself. He'd simply let the sexual chemistry run its course and when it was over, they would both move on with their lives. No, the only one who would be hurt would be Peterson—and the blow would be more to his ego than anything else.

"…and all things considered, I don't think it's in the best interest of the hotel," Laura continued, laying out her reasons for not wanting him there and omitting the primary one; that they had been within minutes of tumbling into bed.

Despite her all-business attitude, the sexual tension was still there—like the proverbial pink elephant in the middle of a room that no one admitted to seeing. He could see it though. It was there in the way she avoided eye contact with him, in the way she seemed unable to remain still, in the way she tensed each time he came within a few feet of her. And from the shadows under her eyes, he suspected he wasn't the only one who'd had trouble sleeping last night. Not even a cold shower had been able to stop him from thinking about her, from wanting her. He still wanted her. Fortunately, he knew how to control that wanting and not allow it to control him and interfere with his business.

Unlike his father.

An image flashed through Jack's mind of his father sitting alone in the dark with a drink in his hand. His father had made the mistake of letting sentiment override his business sense and look what it had cost him. Samuel Hawke had lost not only his wife and company when Nicole had taken off with his business partner, but he'd also lost his will to live. He had learned from his father's mistakes, Jack reminded himself. He had no intention of letting that happen to him—regardless of how tempting he found Laura Spencer. Bedding Laura and shoving it in his stepbrother's face would be a fringe benefit, one that he would enjoy. But he wouldn't put it or her before business. No, business would always come first. That was why he'd decided to get the due diligence on a fast track, so that when the thirty-day proviso was up, he'd be ready to close the deal and set his plans for the hotel in motion. Whether those plans included Laura or not would be up to her.

"...so if you'll just give me a list of what reports and information you need to perform the due diligence, I'll see that they're sent to your suite."

Tuning back in to what Laura was saying, Jack caught only the tail end of her remark. But it was enough for him to know that she was still balking at giving him a work space in the corporate offices. "Maybe you didn't hear me the first time," Jack said, his voice firm. "I have no intention of working from my suite. I need an office, preferably one on this floor where the data is more accessible. It's all spelled out there in the letter from my attorney," he said, referring to the document he had returned to her. He walked around the desk and picked up the letter. Holding it up, he pointed to the appropriate clause. "According to those terms, the Contessa

Hotel and its representative, that's you, will provide Hawke Industries and/or its representative, which is me, adequate office space to perform the due-diligence portion of the contract."

Laura snatched the letter from him, crumpled it in her fist. "I know what it says. I can read. But I can't give you what I don't have. There is no office available," she argued. "So you're just going to have to suck it up and work out of your suite like you've been doing."

"Wrong. I have no intention of spending my time coming down here to access data or having you send the information upstairs to me," he told her. "Even you have to agree that would be a waste of valuable time for both of us."

"I do agree. But I don't see where you have any choice. There is no office available."

"Then I suggest you make one available," Jack insisted.

"And just how am I supposed to do that?" she snapped.

"You're a smart woman. Figure something out.

After all, you're the one who insisted we play by the rules, remember?" he pointed out, referring to the thirty-day grace period in the contract that she'd insisted on exercising. "The rules say I get an office."

"Anyone ever tell you what a jerk you are?"

"Repeatedly," he said.

She sat down in her chair, shoved the hair back from her face. After letting out a breath, she looked up at him again and said, "All right. Since I want as few people as possible to know why you're here, you can have my office."

"Where are you going to work?"

"What difference does it make? You're getting your office."

"It makes a difference because you're the hotel's general manager, at least for the time being, and I need you to run this place. After the foreclosure if you don't want to stay on, I'll bring someone else in to take over. But until then, your contract says that you're the GM. So I repeat, where are you going to work?"

She looked mad enough to chew nails, Jack

thought. "I'll just work out of one of the suites—the way I wanted you to do."

He didn't want to displace the woman, he admitted. She also had a point about not wanting to ignite the rumor mill about the hotel's new ownership—at least not until he had finished his assessments and was ready to take the appropriate action. In the post-Katrina climate, staffing remained a problem citywide and he didn't want to lose valuable employees needlessly. "That won't work. You need to be here."

"Well, I don't see where I have a lot of choices. As you pointed out, I have to provide you with an office. Since there's none available, someone has to give up theirs and it's not going to be one of my staff. Your being here to supposedly conduct an evaluation of the hotel's operations for marketing purposes is going to raise enough questions. So the only option is for you to take my office."

"Then we'll share the office."

She blinked, evidently stunned by the suggestion. "You've got to be kidding."

"I seldom kid," he told her. Shoving aside a pile of folders, Jack sat on the edge of her desk. He didn't miss the sudden tension in her body at his close proximity. Nor did he miss the awareness that crept into her eyes. He'd seen it last night when she'd realized he was wearing nothing more than a towel. He'd watched desire cloud her anger. And watching her had fed his own hunger for her. The memory set off a sharp jab of need as he recalled how she'd tasted, how her hands had felt on his skin.

"The idea is ridiculous," she told him and averted her gaze.

Annoyed with himself and with her, Jack shut off the memories and stood. Determined to focus on business, he picked up the amethyst paperweight from her desk, tested its weight in his palm. "What's ridiculous is for either one of us to work out of a suite when this office is more than big enough for the two of us. And since a lot of the information I'll need will have to come from you, it makes sense for us to both work out of here."

"That may sound good in theory, but—"

"Would you rather have me in an office where someone might overhear me on the phone and learn something they shouldn't? If I'm working from here, neither one of us has still to worry about that happening." He paused, gave her a moment to digest the idea.

"I guess it could work," she conceded, reluctance in her voice. "But…"

"But what, Laura?" he countered, irritated by her refusal to look at him. "What's the real reason you don't want me here?"

Finally, she looked at him and the coolness was back in her green eyes. "Besides the fact that you're trying to steal my family's hotel, I don't want you here because I don't trust you."

Her words hit him like fists. Angry, he walked over to her and said, "Is it really me you don't trust, Laura? Or is it yourself? Could it be you're worried that if we're alone together we'll finish what we started last night?"

"That monster-size ego of yours is showing again, Hawke."

"My ego has nothing to do with it. You and I

both know that you wanted me every bit as much as I wanted you last night. And the only reason you didn't wake up in my bed this morning is because you got cold feet."

She pushed away from the desk and stood, taking a step back and putting distance between them. "I didn't get cold feet. I came to my senses. Last night I was tired after my trip and I was upset and wasn't thinking clearly. What happened was a mistake."

Her mention of her trip to California, coupled with her denial, angered him even more. "Is that what it was?" he asked as he moved closer, crowding her personal space. "When you had your hot little hands all over my body and my tongue was in your mouth, that was a mistake?"

"Yes," she insisted. "And it's one I have no intention of repeating."

"Then tell me, sweet Laura. Just how do you intend to pay off on our bet when you lose? Because you are going to lose. And when you do, I intend to collect."

* * *

"I can't tell you how much I appreciate this and I promise I'll pay you back just as soon as I can arrange refinancing of the hotel," Laura told her former stepfather, who had just called to inform her he'd wired five hundred thousand dollars to her account.

"You just pay me back when you can and come for another visit soon," Vincent Vincenzo told her. "Be sure to say hello to your mother for me. *Ciao.*"

"*Ciao.*" Laura hung up the phone and leaned back in her chair. A range of emotions rushed through her. Relief. Gratitude. Love. Regardless of all the chaos her parents brought into her life with their merry-go-round of marriages, she had definitely been the lucky one because she had ended up with a wonderful extended family.

Grateful to have the office to herself for a change, Laura retrieved the plan she'd devised to come up with the money to pay off her mother's note. She added the loan from her stepfather to the list and studied the totals. Thanks to Chloe signing over her stock to her, she'd used it and her own stock as collateral on a four-million-dollar loan from another bank. Of course, the interest rate was outrageous. But she'd been desperate and had agreed to the terms. She'd netted another two hundred fifty thousand by cashing in her stocks, IRAs and savings account. Her accountant had warned her that the tax penalties would be a killer, but a big tax bill was the least of her worries at the moment. With the one hundred fifty grand she'd gotten from her own father and the one hundred grand from Chloe's dad, she had managed to come up with five million dollars. Now all she needed was for her mother to be successful in refinancing the nightclub for at least ten million dollars and she would have the fifteen million she needed to cure the defaulted loan.

Then the hotel and its stock would be returned to her family and Jackson Hawke would be out of her office, out of her hotel and out of her life. So why did the prospect of never seeing Jack again leave her feeling more unsettled than pleased? Not sure she wanted to examine the reasons too closely, Laura returned her finance plan to her drawer and dove into the weekly reports. She was still going through the reports when Jack entered the office.

In the nearly two weeks that they had shared an office, he had done nothing to be overly intrusive. His phone conversations were brief. His questions minimal. His interruptions few. He had made no further references to their bet. Nor had he attempted to kiss her again. Yet she had been keenly aware of his presence. The tension between them had been like a live wire dangling in a storm, leaving her on edge, waiting for the sparks to ignite. And each time she looked across the room and found his eyes on her, the desire she saw in them made her blood heat.

It simply made no sense. While she was no prude, sex wasn't something she took lightly. She'd only slept with two men in her life—her first love and Matt Peterson. In each case, she'd known the man for nearly a year and had strong feelings for him before she'd shared his bed.

She'd known Jack for less than a month and the feelings he aroused in her were certainly not feelings of love. Yet, there was no denying her physical attraction to him. The admission worried her as much as it annoyed her.

"Isn't there someone else who can generate a copy of the report?"

Laura looked up at the sound of Jack's voice and glanced over to the table where he had been working. He'd shed the dark suit coat and silk tie he'd worn that morning, she noted. The crisp white shirt was open at the collar. The gold cuff links at his wrists caught the light as he put down his pen. Sitting back in his chair, he shoved a hand through his hair, and Laura couldn't help remembering sliding her own fingers through his damp hair that night in his hotel suite.

"All right, then. Just leave a message for him to call me when he gets in," Jack said and hung up the phone.

"Is there a problem?" she asked.

"I'm missing the copy of the marketing projections for the first quarter of next year and the guy who handles it took off this afternoon to go to see his daughter in a school Christmas pageant."

She smiled. "Jerry's daughter is in kindergarten and she's an angel in the pageant. I told him he could have the afternoon off," she told him. "But I should have a copy of the report you can use."

A few minutes later, after she'd located the report and handed it to him, he said, "Thanks."

"No problem." Curious, she asked, "So how is the due diligence coming? Have you been able to get everything you needed?"

"It's going pretty well. And yes, so far I've been able to get or access all the data I've asked for."

"How much longer do you think it'll take before you finish?"

His lips twitched. "What's the matter? Tired of sharing your office or just anxious to get rid of me?"

"Both."

He chuckled. "At least you're honest."

"You asked."

This time he actually laughed aloud. And

Laura realized it was the first time she had heard him laugh since that night in the park. She couldn't help thinking that despite his fortune and power, Jack didn't seem to have a lot of laughter in his life. Or people, she realized. While he had lots of employees, she could never recall him mentioning any family or close friends.

"You're right. I did ask. And in answer to your question, it should only take me another week, maybe less to finish." He sat back, stretched his arms behind his head and looked up at her. "How about you? Any problems with the employees buying the story about me doing a marketing analysis?"

"Not really. Some people are curious and there have been a few questions," she advised him. Most of those questions had come from the accounting department, which she had expected since the info that Jack had requested was much more expansive than the data needed for marketing purposes. "But they seemed satisfied with the explanation I had Penny give them. And it hasn't been a secret that I'm trying to increase the hotel's revenues. They think that you're part of that plan."

"I guess I am, in a manner of speaking, if things go down as I plan."

"But not if they go as I've planned."

"True," he said with a smile. "Other than for the obvious reason that your family owned this hotel, why a career in hotel management?"

The question surprised her. It was the first time in nearly two weeks that he'd spoken to her about anything that didn't relate to the hotel's operation. "The truth is, I knew from the time I was a little girl that I wanted to be a hotelier. More specifically, I wanted to run this hotel." For the next fifteen minutes she told him about how enamored she had been by her grandfather's stories about the people who had stayed in the hotel, how he had taught her that each person was like a guest in their home. She told him how for nearly a hundred years the lives and loves of countless people had played out within the walls of the Contessa, that the hotel stood as a witness to history. "Did you know that an Austrian duke once stayed here?"

"A duke, huh?"

"Yes. It was in the early 1930s when my great-grandfather was running the hotel. Anyway, the duke and his consort were here for the Mardi Gras festivities. In particular, they were special guests attending the meeting of the courts of Rex and Comus on Mardi Gras night," she explained, telling him about the momentous occasion that had, for nearly a century, signaled the final events of the holiday. "They supposedly chose to stay at the Contessa because of it's old-world charm."

"That must have been quite a coup for your great-grandfather."

"It was. In fact, there's a photograph of him and my grandfather with the duke and duchess hanging over there." She stood and walked over to the wall in question where the photo from the bygone era was displayed.

"I assume the serious little boy is your grand-father," he said from behind her.

"Yes, and the man wearing the costume and mask is my great-grandfather, Robert Spencer," she said, and was surprised to turn and find Jack standing so close to her. Disarmed by his nearness, Laura returned her attention to the photograph and adjusted it.

"Is that your grandfather, too?" he asked, indicating another shot of a young man in a doorman's uniform, smiling and holding the door for guests. After assuring him the young man was indeed her grandfather, he said, "He certainly looks like he's enjoying his job."

"He did. My grandfather loved this place. Instead of having bedtime stories read to me as a child, I got stories about movie stars and royals and even bank robbers who had stayed here. I knew that I wanted to have my own stories to tell my children and grandchildren someday," she said wistfully and traced her fingers over the photo before turning. "What about you? What did you want to be when you grew up?"

"Rich."

Surprised, she thought he was kidding and

said, "What happened to wanting to be a fireman or a cowboy?"

"They don't make enough money."

Again surprised by his response, she asked, "And just how old were you when you reached that conclusion?"

"Six."

He said it so matter-of-factly, she realized he was serious. She couldn't help wondering what had happened to him at six that would have had him set such a serious goal. So she asked, "What was so important about being rich?"

"Because when you're rich, people like you better. They want to be around you. They're nice to you because they know you have money and can buy them things, can take them places," he said.

"Having people hang out with you just for your money doesn't sound all that great to me. It certainly isn't the kind of friends that I would want."

"Maybe not," he said, a sardonic note in his voice. "But it sure beats people treating you like a loser because you don't have money or ditching you for somebody else who does."

Judging by the hard look in his eyes, Laura was sure Jack was speaking from personal experience. And the realization made her feel sad for him. "What they say is true, Jack. Money isn't everything."

"Sure it is. Money is power. And power is all that really matters."

"So is that why you do what you do? Buy companies like the Contessa for the power?"

"That's a big part of it," he conceded. "But there's also the challenge of turning a company around and making it profitable."

"So that you can make more money," she added drily.

"Yes."

"But where's the joy in that? Where's the passion?"

"The joy is in being able to make it happen. As for the passion, I find all the passion I need with the woman who's in my bed. You're the woman I would have found that passion with if you hadn't run out on me." He edged a step closer, cupped the back of her head with his hand.

"Jack," she said, her voice suddenly dry. Despite her attempts to resist him, Laura could feel her pulse start to stutter.

"You can still be that woman, Laura," he told her as he brushed his mouth against hers. "I want you."

She pressed her hands against his chest, unsure if she intended to push him away or draw him closer. He slid his hand down her back, drew her to him, and the feel of his arousal sent waves of heat through her.

"All you have to do is say yes and we can go to my suite now. Then I'll show you what real passion is."

She was tempted. Oh, she was tempted, Laura admitted as he kissed her jaw, moved to her neck. The nip of his teeth to her sensitive flesh sent a shiver of need through her body.

"Laura." Penny buzzed through on the intercom. "I have Matt Peterson on line one for you."

It took Laura a moment before she registered the sudden stiffening of Jack's body or the way the hand that had been caressing her was now curled into a fist in her jacket. But that momentary cease in the assault to her senses was enough for Laura to catch her breath and realize where she was, what she was doing and who she was doing it with. The realization that Penny or anyone could have walked in on them was like a sobering blast of cold air. She eased back from him and his hands fell away. "I really need to take this call," she said.

"Right," he told her, his voice cool, his expression shuttered. And before she could say another word, his back was to her. After shoving his laptop into its case, he snapped it shut, then grabbed his jacket and started for the door. "When you make up your mind, you know where to find me."

Seven

"Hello, Matt," Laura said as she stared at the door through which Jack had exited so abruptly.

"Hi, beautiful. How are you?"

"Fine," she said absently, her thoughts still on Jack and his swift change of mood. "How about you?"

"Much better now that I've finally reached you."

At his sweet declaration, Laura shoved thoughts of Hawke from her mind and thought about Matt. An image of his face filled her mind's eye. Tall, blond and brown-eyed, Matt Peterson had Brad Pitt good looks and a double dose of charisma. A partner in a major law firm in L.A., he was smart, civic-minded and a man of action. He was sexy, exciting and fun to be with. In short, he was everything she thought she wanted in a man. And even though she cared deeply for him, she didn't love him—not with the deep-rooted passion she'd seen her parents find with their partners, but mostly not with the unshakable love that her grandparents had shared for one another.

"You're a hard woman to reach, babe. Have you been getting my messages?"

"Yes, I got them. And I'm sorry for not calling you back. It's just that I've been swamped and haven't had a moment to spare." It wasn't entirely true, she admitted silently. While the problems at the hotel and Hawke had eaten up most of her time, she hadn't called Matt back because she simply hadn't wanted to go another round with him about her returning to California.

"Sounds to me like you need a vacation. Why don't you take a break and come out here this weekend for a visit? It's been too long since I've seen you, Laura. I miss you."

"I can't, Matt. I've got too much going on here right now."

"Is there a problem?" he asked. "You sound… on edge."

His remark reminded Laura how perceptive Matt could be. For a moment, she considered telling him about the problem with Hawke, her mother's note and the impending foreclosure on the hotel. He was an attorney and businessman from an affluent family and could probably help her secure the funding she needed. But something told her the price he'd expect in return for his help would be too high. Matt wanted a socialite wife like his mother, a woman to adorn his arm, host his parties and be devoted to him and his interests. While some women would be happy in that role, she knew that she wouldn't. Even if that weren't the case, she would still be reluctant to tell him about Hawke. The thing with Hawke had turned personal and she didn't trust that Matt wouldn't sense the truth. It didn't matter that Matt had dated others since her departure and done so with her blessing. Matt was far too competitive to view her interest in Hawke as anything other than a threat to him. If he knew how close she had come to sleeping with Hawke, he'd see it as a challenge to his manhood. And the last thing she wanted was to deal with Matt's ego.

"Laura, is everything all right?"

"Yes. I'm just tired," she told him, which was the truth—if only part of it.

"I told you going down there and trying to salvage that old place was a mistake. You're wearing yourself out. You should have stayed here in California."

"I didn't want to stay in California," she reminded him. "And I really don't want to argue with you about this again."

"I'm sorry, babe. I just hate the thought of you pushing yourself so hard. I worry about you."

"I know," she said with a sigh because she knew that he did care about her. And for the first time, she wondered if maybe she should have just ended things as she'd wanted to do six months ago instead of allowing Matt to convince her that they could still remain a part of each other's lives. If her move had done nothing else, it had confirmed her realization that she didn't want a future with Matt as anything more than a friend. Of course, this crazy attraction to Hawke certainly proved that she could never love Matt.

"Listen, I know you're too busy to come back now. But Christmas is only a couple of weeks away. What do you say you come spend Christmas here in L.A., then we'll drive up to see my parents at their place in Big Bear and do some skiing. I know they'd love to see you."

"It all sounds wonderful, Matt. But I can't," she told him, realizing it wouldn't be fair for her to end things with him over the phone. "Chloe's staying with me for a few weeks and I don't want to leave her alone at Christmas."

"All right," he said, an edge in his voice. "Then I guess I'll just have to settle for seeing you after Christmas. In fact, see if you can get into L.A. by the twenty-eighth. One of my backers for the

senatorial race is throwing a big party then to in-
troduce me to some of his friends. And my
parents are hosting their big New Year's Eve
party, so there'll be lots of press coverage."

"I'm afraid I won't be able to make it then,
either," she told him. "I promised Papa Vincenzo
that I'd come see him and Maria and the boys
before the New Year."

"Dammit, Laura. I get your feeling you need
to be with Chloe for Christmas. Even if she is
just your half sister, there's blood there," he said.
"But what I don't get is you blowing off
spending New Year's with me for those…those
people?"

Angry now, Laura said, "Those people happen
to be my family."

"Give me a break. Just because the guy was
married to your mother for a little while doesn't
make them your family. For crying out loud, the
man's your ex-stepfather and his kids are your
ex-stepbrothers. There's no blood tie there.
Those people are nothing to you."

"That's where you're wrong, Matt. Those

people are everything to me." And without waiting for him to reply, she hung up the phone.

Stepping inside of his suite at the hotel, Jack dumped his laptop case and coat on the chair near the door, then tossed his key card onto the table. He wanted to punch something. No, he amended, he wanted to punch *someone*.

Matt Peterson.

Anger ripped through him as he recalled Laura all hot and sweet and soft in his arms only to turn away from him to take his stepbrother's call. It wasn't about her rejecting him, Jack told himself. He could handle rejection. If a woman wasn't into him, that was fine. He certainly didn't lack for female company and finding a woman willing to share his bed had never been a problem. Hell, Laura had been more than willing to share his bed. She had been as hot and eager for him as he had been for her.

Until Peterson had called.

When given the choice, she had walked away from him for Peterson. The son of a rich man, the golden boy that people flocked to, the one his own mother had adopted as her son all those years ago and had preferred over him. The fact that Laura had chosen Peterson over him fed his anger. But beneath that anger there was something else—an ache that felt dangerously close to hurt.

Enraged with himself that he had allowed Laura to affect him so deeply, that he had somehow given her the power to cause him this hurt, Jack stormed through the suite. He pushed open the door to the bathroom, went to the sink and doused his face with cold water. It hit him like a slap and helped clear his head somewhat.

Grabbing a towel, he dried his face and shoved the hair from his eyes. He braced his hands on the sink, drew in a breath. Satisfied he had his emotions under control, he hung the towel on the rack beside the counter. As he did so, memories of Laura flashed through his head. Laura staring at his naked chest, unknotting the towel at his waist. Laura looking at him, her eyes dark with desire, her mouth hot and hungry as she kissed him. Then suddenly it wasn't him Laura was looking at. It wasn't him she was kissing. It was Peterson she was clinging to, Peterson whose name she was gasping.

All the anger came rushing back. Furious with her and with himself, Jack turned away and stalked back into the living area. He headed straight to the bar where he snatched a glass and poured himself two fingers of whiskey. Wrapping his fist around the glass, he brought it to his lips and was about to toss it back when he realized what he was doing. He slammed the glass down on the bar untouched, sending liquor sloshing over the rim. He would not use liquor to numb the anger and pain the way his father had done.

Instead, he did what he always did. He took refuge in his work. Jack wasn't sure how long he worked. Long enough for him to plow through a mountain of e-mails and reports from his various holdings. Long enough for his shoulders to become stiff. Long enough for his stomach to remind him that the minibar snacks he'd fed it during his infrequent breaks weren't doing the job. But the thought of venturing out to dinner held no appeal. Besides, he was on a roll, Jack told himself.

Retrieving his cell phone, he punched in his assistant, Dotty's, home number. The second she answered, he barked out, "I want you to call Jardine's office and tell them to make sure they have everything ready to close on this deal," he said, referring to the attorney handling the sale. "And the minute the thirty days in that default clause are up, I want the deal closed." When she didn't respond, he asked, "Dotty, did you hear me?"

"I heard you," she said. "But if it's okay with you, I'll wait until morning and call Ms. Jardine at the office because I'm guessing she and her family might be getting ready for bed about now."

The sarcasm in her voice wasn't wasted on him. "It's not that late," he told her. But a glance at the clock on the bedside table proved him wrong. It was after ten o'clock, which meant it was even later in New York. The silence that followed was telling. "All right, it is late," he conceded. "And

I'm sorry if I disturbed you. But I want you to call first thing in the morning and tell her—"

"I know. You want the deal closed ASAP. I'll call Ms. Jardine's office in the morning and make sure everything's on track."

"Good. I also want you to make some calls and find out exactly where Laura Spencer stands on raising that money. I know her mother and step-father are trying to refinance the nightclub in Paris. Find out where they are on that." He filled her in on what he already knew. Namely that Chloe had signed over her stock to her sister and Laura had pledged it and her own stock for a loan. He also knew that she had cashed out her stocks and savings. What he didn't know was if Peterson had loaned her the money. "Give Sean Fitzpatrick at Fitzpatrick Investigations a call, too. Have him see if Matt Peterson or his family have made any large cash transactions."

"Jack, you never said anything about your stepbrother being involved in this deal," Dotty told him and he didn't miss the worry in her voice.

"I don't know that he is. But he and the Spencer woman are close friends and I don't want any surprises."

"All right," Dotty told him. "And since I've got you on the phone, what do you want me to tell the people at City Park about that donation you made to restore the carousel? They're most appreciative and want to have a commemorative plaque installed, acknowledging the donation. They also want to hold a press conference to announce Hawke Industries' generosity."

Jack hesitated a minute, then recalled the night Laura had shown him the Carousel Gardens and told him about her grandfather taking her there for the first time. "Tell them the plaque should read In Memory of Oliver Jordan, Hotelier."

"And the press conference?"

"Tell them I want to wait until after the first of the year and have the Contessa Hotel listed as the donor. List Laura Spencer as their contact person."

"Got it," Dotty told him. "Anything else?"

"That's it. Just make sure our people are ready to come in here and get things rolling once this goes down so I can get started on the Henderson's Plastics deal," he said, referring to a company he'd been eyeing in California.

"So you won't be sticking around New Orleans?"

"No. There's no reason for me to stay here once things are under way. Besides, my home is in New York."

"You live in a hotel suite," she reminded him.

"Which has a laundry, a housekeeper and twenty-four-hour room service."

"That's not a home, Jack."

"It's the only home I need. Good night, Dotty." He hit the off button on the phone. Annoyed by his assistant's remark, Jack went over to the minibar, grabbed a can of nuts and a bottle of water. He popped the top on the can of nuts, ate a handful and then washed it down with water. As he munched on the snack, he looked around the luxurious room.

There wasn't a thing wrong with living in a hotel, he told himself. Living in a hotel suited him just fine. There was no fuss, no maintenance, no lawn to cut and a hot meal was only a phone call away. If it felt a little empty or pristine at times, so what? Besides, he wasn't there all that much anyway.

Polishing off the rest of the nuts, Jack walked over to the window and drew open the drapes to look out at the city. The threat of rain that had lingered all day had finally arrived and fell steadily on the streets below. The sky was starless thanks to the dark clouds. Even the moon struggled to be seen through the rainfall and clouds. The streets below were nearly empty, save for an occasional car. Jack suspected that the lack of traffic had more to do with people's lingering fears of flooding in the aftermath of Hurricane Katrina than it had to do with the actual threat of a rainstorm. He couldn't help feeling empathy for the people who had lived through the nightmare and had bravely returned.

Since the stormy weather suited his mood, Jack left the drapes open. After trading his dress slacks and shirt for a pair of jeans, a shirt and sweater, he returned to the table and his laptop where he went back to work. He was knee-deep in the projected operating budget for the hotel when he looked for the report that detailed the operating expenses for the prior five years and realized he didn't have it. Evidently, he had left it in Laura's office when he'd stormed out that afternoon. Still too restless to call it a night, Jack took the elevator downstairs to the executive office to retrieve the report.

Exiting the elevator, he started down the hall toward the office. He had the key to the door in his hand when he reached the suite of offices and found it unlocked. When he entered the reception area, he spied the light shining from Laura's office. The door was ajar and he could hear her speaking to someone.

"Yes, I know," she said. "I know that, too."

She was on the phone, he realized, and felt that punch in his gut again as he remembered who she had been speaking to when he'd left her this afternoon. Refusing to allow himself to go down that road again, Jack reminded himself he was there to get a file. He pushed the door open and walked over to the table.

Laura turned as he entered and there was no mistaking the surprise on her face. Lightning flashed outside the window behind her, illuminating her face. Her skin was pale, her eyes huge. She'd repaired the damage to her hair and lipstick that he'd done earlier, but it did little to disguise her fatigue.

"I'd better go, Mother. It looks like this storm is turning nasty. I should probably head home before it gets worse," Laura said.

It was her mother, Jack realized. Annoyed with himself because he was pleased that it hadn't been Peterson she was talking to, he began searching through the files for the report he needed.

"Yes, I understand. Just let me know as soon as you hear."

So her mother still hadn't been able to get the refinancing on the nightclub, he surmised. Did that mean Peterson hadn't come through for her yet? Even if his stepbrother didn't have that kind of money himself to lend her, his parents certainly did. It would take moving some stocks or pledging other assets, but Edward and Nicole Peterson were very wealthy people and they had never denied his son anything. Too bad the same couldn't be said for her son. But then, Jack had stopped being Nicole's son a long time ago, he reminded himself. All he was to her was a reminder that she had once been married to a loser.

"I will, Mother. Yes. I love you, too," Laura said and hung up the phone. After a moment, she said, "Jack, I'm sorry about…about earlier."

"Don't sweat it. I didn't," he told her and continued rummaging through the files.

"No, I guess you wouldn't," she tossed back.

There was something in her voice, a weariness beneath the sharp retort that caused him to look over at her. She looked sad and confused and vulnerable. But it was the sadness that touched something inside him, something he didn't want her to touch. And because she had the ability to make him feel, he resented her for it. Unable to locate the report he wanted, Jack dumped all the files into the briefcase he had left on the table. He'd take them all back to his suite

and look for the one he needed there, he decided.
Another bolt of lightning streaked through the
sky. Thunder boomed. The lights flickered and
he jerked his gaze up. "How good is the backup
generator?"

"Good enough."

"When was the last time it was serviced?"

"I don't know the exact date. But it was
sometime last year, shortly before I took over
management," she told him as she began
shutting down her own computer system. "We
haven't had a major storm since Hurricane
Katrina."

But he knew that the backup generator was
old. In fact, according to the records, it had been
retired and designated as the backup more than
ten years ago when a new generator had been
purchased. Given the difficulties experienced in
restoring power to the ravaged city, he wasn't
sure that either generator could sustain a minor
storm, let alone a major one. And this one
sounded like a big one if that last blast of thunder
meant anything. "You may want to rethink trying

to get home in that mess and take a room here for tonight."

"I'll be fine," she assured him as she switched off her desk lamp and gathered her briefcase and purse. When she reached the door, Jack allowed her to precede him and then he followed her out. After locking up the offices, they walked in silence down the corridor to the elevator banks. Jack punched the up button. She pressed the one for down. And they waited.

And waited.

She punched the button again. So did he. But according to the floor indicator, both elevators continued to move at a snail's pace. "I'll just take the stairs," he told her.

"Jack, wait," she said when he started for the stairwell door. "That's a lot of stairs. I'm going to take the freight elevator. If you don't mind riding down to the first floor with me first, you can use it to go up to the penthouse."

"Sounds good to me," he told her and followed her down to the far end of the hallway where the elevator the staff used for servicing the guest floors was tucked in a corner. Within moments of pressing the button, the elevator doors opened and they stepped inside.

Laura hit the down button for the first floor and the elevator started to descend.

Jack watched as the car lumbered down, passing the fifth floor, then the fourth floor. And then the elevator slammed to a halt, nearly knocking Laura off her high heels. Jack caught her arm to keep her from falling forward.

"Thanks," she murmured as she straightened herself. Then she hit the button for the first floor again.

Nothing happened.

When she tried three more times and the car failed to move, she said, "What in the devil's wrong with this thing?"

Jack frowned. "What's wrong is it's stuck. And so are we."

Eight

Stuck?

They couldn't be stuck, Laura told herself. The elevator was just having a little hiccup. That was all. No way was she stuck in this elevator with Jack. "It'll start again in a minute," she said more to herself than to him. She set her briefcase and purse down on the floor and punched the floor buttons—all of them.

Nothing happened.

"I told you, it's stuck. Try pushing the emergency lever."

She tried. But still nothing happened. She

pulled open the door to the red emergency box that contained the phone only to find that someone had cut the phone cord. Laura could feel her heart begin to race. Telling herself there was no reason to panic, she snatched her purse from the floor. "I'll just call the front desk on my cell phone," she said and began digging through the handbag. When she located it, she flipped it open. "No signal," she told him. "Either the storm took out the satellite or the walls of the elevator are interfering with the reception. You'll need to call the hotel on your phone."

Jack reached for the clip on his belt, but it was empty. "I left it in my suite."

Her stomach sank at the news. She was in trouble. She was alone with Jack in a space the size of a small closet. And no one even knew she was there. Not Chloe. Not her assistant, Penny. Not any of the hotel staff. The realization sent a wave of panic rushing through her. She had to get out of here. She had to, Laura told herself and she began slapping at the buttons again.

"Hey, take it easy," Jack told her as he caught

her hands, holding them in his fists. When she started to struggle, he narrowed his eyes. "What's wrong? Are you claustrophobic?"

"No," she responded. But as she looked around, noting just how small the elevator was, she felt even more trapped. The air suddenly seemed thin, as though she were on a high mountaintop. "At least I wasn't until you mentioned it," she told him, both annoyed and scared. Pulling her hands free, she tried her phone again.

"It's okay," he told her.

Laura ignored him. Struggling to breathe, she tried to fight off the growing panic while she continued to hit at the buttons on the panel. She had to get out. She had to get out. She repeated the words silently like a litany.

"Laura," he said.

When she failed to respond, he stepped in front of her. But with the tide of panic sweeping through her and her breathing growing more difficult by the minute, she struck at him. Her blows seemed to bounce off his chest, but still she continued to fight him to get to the control panel. She needed to get the door open. She needed to get out of the elevator.

Jack caught her fists, sandwiched them between his palms and held them. "Laura. Laura," he repeated her name softly. "Breathe. Try to breathe."

It was the gentle way he had said her name that eased some of her panic. No longer struggling, she drew a deep breath, released it. As her heart rate slowed, so did her breathing. She looked up at Jack, stared into blue eyes that were warm, caring, concerned.

"It's okay," he told her gently.

But it wasn't okay. It might never be okay again, she thought. She was running out of time to get the money and her mother's attempts to refinance the nightclub had been turned down by two banks already. Her hopes of retaining the Contessa were on the verge of sinking and had a great deal to do with her stressed-out state. The ugly conversation with Matt and the realization that their relation-ship was nearly over had only added to what had turned into a lousy day. But it was the knowledge that she was swimming in dangerous waters on a personal level where Jack was concerned that worried her the most. She didn't want to be attracted to him. She didn't want to want him. And she didn't want to like him, to care about him. Even if the Contessa was not an issue between them, the emotional risks were far too great. Jackson Hawke was not a man who believed in love and commitment. He'd made that abundantly clear. And she… She was a woman who believed in and wanted both. To be trapped in an elevator with him was only asking for trouble that she didn't need, that she wasn't sure she could handle. That night in his hotel suite had proven that. So had this afternoon in her office. Had it not been for Matt's call, she wasn't at all sure she would have called a halt to things.

"Better?" he asked.

She nodded, drew another steadying breath. "You can let me go now."

He hesitated a moment, then released her. "I don't think it was a power outage. The light in here is still working. It's probably just the elevator."

Thinking more clearly, she noted that the light was indeed still working and told herself that was one thing for which she could be grateful. Otherwise, they would be trapped together in the dark. She waited, expecting him to remind her what poor condition the entire elevator system was in, but he didn't. Probably because he knew that she was well aware of it already. "It still doesn't change the fact that the car is stuck."

"No. But it means the rest of the hotel has power. The next time someone goes to use the service elevator, they'll discover it isn't working and report it to the maintenance department. Once maintenance is aware there's a problem, they'll correct it and get the car running again. Then we'll be able to get out."

"That would be fine except for the fact that no one's likely to discover the elevator isn't working until morning. It's after eleven o'clock. Room service stopped fifteen minutes ago and most of the housekeeping staff are gone for the day," she explained. "The chance that anyone will even try to use this elevator before morning is very slim."

"Maybe. Maybe not," he conceded. "The front-desk staff know you're still in the hotel. They might be used to you keeping long hours, but when you don't leave, someone's bound to come looking for you."

Laura shook her head. "There was a shift change two hours ago. I doubt anyone knows I'm still here. If they do, they'll think I just decided to spend the night on the couch in my office. I've done that before."

"What about Chloe? She's staying with you, isn't she? She'll come looking for you when you don't come home," he reasoned.

Laura would have laughed if she hadn't felt so dismayed. "Her stepsister, Meredith Grant, was arriving this evening for that meeting Chloe conned you into taking to discuss Meredith's company. Tonight Chloe was introducing Meredith to the city's nightlife. Knowing my sister, her chance of getting in before dawn is about as good as my chance of winning the lottery."

"What about your friend Peterson, the one you had to take the call from this afternoon?" he asked, an edge in his voice. "Won't he get worried when he calls you tonight and can't reach you?"

"Matt won't be calling me," she said firmly. Knowing Matt as she did, he would see nothing wrong in what he'd said and would expect her to make the next move by apologizing to him. "So unless someone is expecting you, no one knows we're missing."

"No one's expecting me," he told her, and Laura could have sworn the hardness that she'd detected a moment ago was gone.

"Then that means we're stuck here for at least…" she glanced at her watch and continued "…the next five hours, maybe six, depending on when someone needs to use the service elevator."

"In that case, I suggest we make ourselves comfortable."

"What do you think you're doing?" she asked as he sat down on the floor and leaned against the wall.

"I told you. I'm getting comfortable. So should you."

"Aren't you going to at least try to get us out of here?" she asked, wondering if the man had lost his mind. Didn't he realize they were trapped in an elevator and no one knew they were there?

He glanced up at her. "And just what is it you expect me to do? The alarm on this thing is shot. I don't have my cell phone and yours won't work. And you said yourself that we're going to have to wait until one of the staff comes along and discovers the elevator is broken."

"But that won't be until morning," she pointed out.

"Precisely. That's why the smart thing for both of us to do is to try to get comfortable while we wait," he said and stretched out one leg while he bent the other. Leaning his head against the wall, he closed his eyes.

Irritated with him and frustrated by the situation, Laura looked around, then up at the tiled ceiling of the car. She knew that there were pulleys on the elevator car that were checked whenever the system was serviced. Through the ceiling, they could also get access to the next floor.

Opening his eyes, he followed the direction of her gaze. "You've got to be kidding," he said, sitting up.

"Why? If you get up on top of the car, you can crawl up to the next floor and get out through one of the vents in the elevator shaft." At his look of skepticism, she added, "It's done all the time."

"In the movies, maybe. But not in real life. Forget it. No way am I going to climb around in that elevator shaft and risk falling and breaking my neck. I can wait until morning for someone to find us."

"Well, I can't wait," she told him. But there was no way she could make it up to the ceiling without help. "All right. I'll do it. You just need to give me a boost up so I can reach the ceiling."

He looked at her as if she'd lost her mind. "In that outfit? You've got to be joking. That skirt isn't exactly made for climbing."

He was right. The skirt's straight cut was

designed to showcase her legs, not for climbing around in an elevator shaft. "Then you go."

"No." He said the word firmly.

"Why not?"

"Because I don't like heights, okay?"

The admission stunned her. Jack had struck her as a man who feared nothing. Learning he had a fear of heights made him more real somehow and reminded her of the tender man she'd spent time with in the park. "I'm sorry. I didn't realize. I'll do it then. All you have to do is help me get up there."

He muttered something about stubborn women and pushed himself up to his feet. "You know, I should let you do it and just sit back and enjoy the view. But I'd hate like hell seeing you break your pretty neck and cheat me out of that night of sex you're going to owe me."

Ignoring the reference to their bet, she said, "Jack, I said I'll do it."

He pulled off his sweater, handed it to her. "Hold this."

Feeling unfair to have pressured him if he

actually was afraid of heights, she said, "Really, Jack. Maybe you should let me go up."

"I said I'd do it," he told her. He stared up at the ceiling tiles for several months, then down at her briefcase. "How sturdy is that briefcase?"

"Very," she said.

"I'm going to need you to hold it as steady as you can while I stand on it so I can reach the ceiling. You wouldn't happen to have a flashlight in there, would you?"

"No, but I've got a penlight," she said, which she retrieved from the key ring in her purse and handed to him.

"Thanks," he said and slid it into his pocket. He tested his weight on the briefcase. Once. Twice. Then he turned to her. "Ready?"

"Ready."

Jack stood on top of the briefcase again and, stretching upward, he pushed on the cover tile in the ceiling that led to the elevator shaft. Once he had managed to nudge the tile aside, he looked down at her for a moment. "All right. Here goes."

"Jack." When he looked back down at her, she said, "Be careful."

"Don't worry, Laura. I intend to collect on that bet." Then he jumped and the tips of his fingers caught the edge of the opening in the ceiling. He clung to it for several long seconds.

Laura let go of the briefcase and moved beneath him so that she could hold either side of his legs. He glanced down at her. "It's okay," she said at his questioning look. "Use my shoulders to brace your feet."

Jack said nothing. And instead of using the leverage she had offered, he tightened his grip and pulled his body up until his shoulders were inside of the opening. Bracing himself on his elbows, he climbed through the rest of the way. For several moments he just seemed to stay where he was, hovering near the opening.

"Are you okay?"

"Yes," he told her and then he moved.

Laura tried to see inside the opening, but it was too dark. She did see a sliver of light occasionally and assumed it was her penlight. Trying to be patient, but finding the wait interminable, she asked, "Jack? Can you see the air vent yet?"

"Yeah," he yelled. He came back to the opening, knelt on one knee and looked down at her. His expression was grim and there was an odd look in his eyes that quickly turned to one of determination. "It's dark as sin inside this thing. But it looks like we're caught between floors. The nearest vent that I can see is a few yards above us. I'm going to see if I can get to it."

"Be careful," she repeated her earlier warning, but she wasn't sure Jack heard her because he had already disappeared back into the dark shaft.

It seemed as though an eternity passed, during which she heard Jack swear twice. Her heart stopped a moment when she heard something fall down the shaft before she realized that it must be the penlight. Finally, he returned to the opening and lowered himself down into the elevator.

"I'm sorry. I tried, but I couldn't get the thing opened. It's sealed tight," he told her as he brushed off his clothes. He sank to the floor, pressed against the wall. His jeans were dusty. His shirt was torn, his hair mussed. "And I owe you for the penlight. I dropped it."

"Forget about the penlight," she said, too worried by the sight of the gash on his forehead to recognize that he was being facetious. She didn't care about the penlight. She didn't even care about them being stuck in the elevator. What she did care about was the fact that Jack was hurt. "You're bleeding," she told him then grabbed her purse and dug through it for the packet of tissues she always carried.

He touched his forehead, looking surprised when he saw the blood. "Must have hit my head harder than I thought. I couldn't see much after I dropped the penlight."

Laura pushed his hand away and dabbed at the cut with a tissue. She was relieved to see that it wasn't as bad as she had first thought. She held the tissue for several moments to stem the bleeding. When she lifted it again, the flow of blood had lessened. "I've got a couple of Band-Aids in my briefcase. Hold this," she said and took his hand to place it on the wad of tissues. "Try to keep pressure on it while I get them."

"If you happen to have a couple of aspirin in there, I could use them. I've got a killer headache."

She did have aspirin, which she gave to him, along with the bottle of water she had tucked in her purse. Once she had cleaned the cut as best she could with the water and tissues, she placed a bandage over it. Sitting back on her heels, she said, "You've got a knot on your forehead and you're probably going to have an ugly bruise, but I don't think you need stitches."

"So I don't need to worry about looking like Frankenstein, huh?"

She knew the comment was meant to be funny. But she didn't feel the least bit amused. What she felt was guilty because he could have been seriously hurt. "I'm sorry. I should never have insisted you climb into that shaft."

"Hey, you didn't hold a gun to my head," he reminded her.

"I might as well have. The only reason you went in there was because of me." And it was knowing that, realizing it was her fault he was hurt, that he could very easily have fallen or worse, that made her feel even more guilty.

Jack tipped up her chin with his fingertip. "It's just a little scratch, Laura."

"But—"

He pressed his fingers against her lips, silencing her. "I'm fine."

"Are you sure?" she asked him.

"I'm sure," Jack lied. The truth was his head felt as if someone had hit him with a sledgehammer. But Laura looked so worried and guilty, he knew telling her so would make her feel even worse. In an effort to distract her, he said, "Any chance you've got some candy stashed in your purse? My dinner consisted of a raid of the minibar in my room, so I'm starving."

She didn't have any candy in her purse, but she did have some in her briefcase. It was her emergency stash, she explained to him as she divided the cache of chocolate-nut bars, peanut-butter cups and chocolate-covered wafers between them.

"I don't have any cups. I don't mind sharing, if you don't," she told him and offered him the bottle of water. He took it. For the next several minutes they ate in silence and as the silence grew he could see the nerves and guilt settling in again. To distract her he asked, "What's it like having such a big family?"

"Crazy. And wonderful," she told him.

As he hoped, she began to relax as she told him about her large, extended family and spending her summers in New Orleans with her grandfather at the Contessa. "It sounds pretty chaotic, all the moving around, people in and out of your life."

"It was, but in a fun way. Chloe used to say we were gypsies and had relatives in every state. But I didn't mind. I always wanted to be part of a big family and every time one of my parents re-married, I inherited another set of relatives."

"What about when they divorced?" he asked. "Didn't it hurt to lose all those new relatives?"

She grinned. "But I didn't lose them. Chloe and I decided that just because our parents got divorced didn't mean we had to. So we just kept the relatives. At last count I had fifteen grand-parents and eleven brothers and sisters."

"That's a big family, all right."

"What about you?"

"My father died about ten years ago," he told her. But, in truth, Samuel Hawke had died long before then. He'd died the day his wife had left him for Edward Peterson.

"What about your mother?"

"She walked out on us when I was six. She's remarried now and has another son. I haven't seen much of her since the divorce."

"What about your brother? Are you and he close?"

"Hardly," Jack said, a wry smile twisting his lips as he thought of Matt Peterson. "He's my stepbrother. And there's never been anything that even remotely resembles family love between us. In fact, it's just the opposite. He detests me as much as I detest him."

"But why?"

Jack sighed. "I guess a lot of it had to do with my parents' divorce. It was a pretty ugly scene and watching people you love hurt each other, make selfish decisions you don't understand, isn't easy," he said, recalling his devastation back then.

"If you'd rather not talk about it, I understand," Laura told him.

Normally he wouldn't have told her about it. He seldom talked to anyone about that time in his life when his entire world seemed to have fallen apart. But looking at Laura now, recalling how she had shared the Carousel House with him that night, told him about her dreams, it felt somehow right to tell her. "My father had a construction business. Nothing big or fancy, but it supported our family. Then he landed a big contract to build a couple of office parks and hotels. It was great and there was the potential to make a lot of money on the deal. It would have made us rich. But he needed money to get the insurance and bonding. So he turned to an old friend who had hit it big in the real-estate business. He agreed to put up the money my Dad needed in exchange for half of the company."

"So your dad agreed," she added.

"Yes. Everything seemed to be going well for about six months or so. But my dad was gone a lot, busy with the business. And my mother wasn't the type of woman who liked being alone. Anyway, my dad's partner was around a lot and after a while I guess he wasn't content with just half of the business. He wanted my dad's wife, too. And my mother apparently didn't need much persuading. She was more than willing to swap what she considered a life of loneliness and pinching pennies for a life of fun and luxury."

"But what about you?" Laura asked. "She just left you?"

"I didn't want to leave my dad. He needed me," Jack explained as he recalled how difficult those first few years had been. "Besides, her rich new husband was a widower with a young son just a little older than me. Even when she was still married to my dad, she paid a lot of attention to him because he didn't have a mother," he told her, using the explanation his mother had always given him for her doting on Matt.

"Anyway, once they were married, she adopted his son. So I guess you could say she traded me for him."

"But you were still her son," Laura said, her outrage clear.

"My stepbrother didn't think so. Whenever I'd go to visit, it was clear he didn't want me around. And the truth is, I didn't like being around them anyway. I didn't fit in. I just didn't belong." A fact that Matt had made sure he knew, Jack recalled. "After my dad sold his share of the business to them, he and I moved to New York. The visits grew fewer and fewer and eventually they stopped altogether. We haven't seen or spoken to each other in years."

"I'm so sorry, Jack," she said and reached out to touch his hand. "Your mother leaving you and your father like that for someone wealthy, she's the reason you said you wanted to be rich."

"Yes," he admitted. "I thought if I could find a way to make a lot of money and become rich then my mother would come back to us. Pretty stupid thinking, huh?"

"No. It was pretty smart thinking for a six-year-old," she told him. "And I guess it's served you well. Because you are rich now."

Yes, he was rich, Jack thought to himself. Yet, lately, he had felt just as lonely and poor as he had been at six. He looked at Laura, thought about her crazy family, how her mother's selfishness and irresponsibility threatened to take away the hotel Laura loved, how she was willing to risk everything she owned to save something created by her family. Despite all the turmoil and financial strain, it was clear that she felt rich and was confident in her family's love. When she stifled a yawn, he suggested, "We probably ought to try to get some sleep. It's nearly one in the morning."

"Do you think that's a good idea? I mean, you have a head injury. You're not supposed to let someone with a head injury go to sleep."

He half smiled. "I don't think a little bump on the head qualifies as a head injury."

She frowned. "You were bleeding and you've got a knot on your head. As far as I'm concerned, that qualifies as a head injury."

When she stifled another yawn, he said, "All right. I do. But I read somewhere that when someone has a head injury, they can go to sleep. You just need to wake them up every hour to make sure they're okay. So why don't I set the alarm on my watch to go off in an hour. If I don't hear it when it goes off, you will and you can wake me up. How's that sound?"

She seemed to consider that. "I guess that would be okay."

So he set the alarm. Already stretched out on the floor, he leaned his head back against the wall and shut his eyes. She, on the other hand, couldn't seem to get comfortable. He opened one eye, watched her stretch out her legs and put her head back against the wall the way he had. She tried tucking her feet beneath her and crossing her arms over her chest. She tried lying flat on her back and then curling into a ball on her side.

"Come over here," he told her.

Laura flushed. "I'm sorry. I didn't mean to wake you. I don't seem to be able to get comfortable and it feels like it's getting colder."

"Here, put this on," he said and tossed her his sweater.

"What about you? Aren't you cold?"

"Just a little. But I imagine it's going to get colder before the night's over. We might as well use our body heat to keep us both warm. So come on over here." When she hesitated, he said, "You don't have to worry, Laura. Being stuck in a cold elevator with a monster-size headache has pretty much put any thoughts of me having sex with you on the back burner for now."

Evidently taking him at his word, she scooted over to his side of the elevator. And when he opened his arms, she settled her head against his chest. Within moments, she was asleep.

But for him, sleep was a long time in coming. There was no need to reset the alarm on his watch when two o'clock rolled around because he was still awake. He was also still awake at three o'clock and four. And his inability to sleep had little to do with his using the floor as a bed and more to do with the woman whose shapely bottom was pressed against his arousal.

Laura stirred against him, adding to his torment and pleasure. He ached to slide his hand beneath her blouse, to feel the heat of her bare flesh against his palm. But to do so now when she was so vulnerable wouldn't be right, he told himself. He'd promised her she was safe. Besides, how would she feel if he slept with her and then foreclosed on the hotel? She already saw him as her enemy. Would she view her actions as a betrayal to herself and her family? Something told him that she would.

There was also the problem of Matt Peterson. How would she feel if she slept with Jack and then discovered that he was Matt's stepbrother, that he had considered bedding her for revenge? It would devastate her. Ashamed that he had ever thought of using her that way, he promised himself she would never know.

Still restless, she turned so that she was facing him, which drove all thoughts of Matt Peterson from his mind. Jack watched her. He noted the sweep of dark lashes that shielded her eyes, the gentle curve of her cheek, the way her lips parted ever so slightly in sleep. He remembered how soft and warm those lips had felt when he'd kissed her, the way she had tasted of both innocence and sin. The memory sent a sharp stab of desire through him, making him painfully aware of why he had been unable to sleep despite his own exhaustion.

She shifted again, adding to his discomfort. This time when she settled, she placed her hand trustingly against his chest. And then she opened her eyes.

Nine

Laura wasn't sure what had awakened her. One moment she'd been dreaming about riding on the carousel and the next moment she'd been under the oak trees in the park with Jack. Then his arms had been around her, pulling her close, engulfing her in the most delicious warmth. And when she had tipped her face up to him, desire had pooled in her belly as he'd watched her out of deep blue eyes that were hot, hungry.

Opening her eyes now, she stared into those same hungry blue eyes. His arms were wrapped around her with one of his hands cupping her rear and one of his legs resting between her thighs. A hard warmth pressed against her belly and heat spread through her like lava as she realized it was Jack's arousal. Suddenly the events of the previous night came rushing back. Being trapped in the elevator. Her panic. Jack soothing her and sharing with her painful memories about his past. Something told her that Jackson Hawke was not a man who shared much of himself with anyone. That he had shared it with her touched something deep inside her.

"Good morning," he said.

"Is it morning yet?" she asked and was surprised how rusty her voice sounded.

Without removing his arm from around her, Jack slanted a glance at the watch on his wrist. "Technically, it is. It's just after six. But the sun probably won't be up for at least another hour. You sleep okay?" he asked.

"Yes," she admitted, surprised by just how soundly she'd slept. Then she remembered the alarm. "I didn't hear the alarm."

"I did," he assured her. "I dutifully reset it for an early hour."

"Did you sleep at all?"

"A little."

But she suspected that wasn't true. There were shadows under his eyes and a tension in his body that told her he'd probably not slept at all. Whiskers darkened his jawline and an ugly bruise spread from beneath the bandage. "How's the head?"

"The jackhammer that was beating in it stopped a couple of hours ago."

She reached up, tested the area around the bandage with her fingertips. "It doesn't look as swollen. But you definitely have a bruise and probably a concussion," she told him. "You should have a doctor look at it once we get out of here."

"I will," he promised.

A wave of tenderness washed through her. She hadn't wanted to desire this man. She certainly hadn't wanted to care for him. He was her enemy, the man who threatened the hotel she loved so dearly. And yet she did want him with an intensity that shocked her. Worse, she was beginning to care for him—more than she should. More than was safe.

But then she had never been one to play it safe, Laura reminded herself. She didn't want to play it safe now. She smoothed her fingers down his face, felt the prickle of his whiskers against her skin, heard him draw in a breath. When he caught her fingers, a thrill went through her as she realized that her very touch had excited him.

"We've probably got at least another hour before someone discovers the elevator is out of commission and finds us. Why don't you try to go back to sleep?"

"I don't want to sleep," she told him. "Do you?"

Heat flashed in those blue eyes. "No."

"Then what do you want to do?"

"This," he said and kissed her mouth.

Excitement swept through her at the feel of his mouth on hers. Her skin burned everywhere his lips touched. He tasted of heat. He tasted of danger. He tasted of need.

When Jack's hands sloped her body, cupped

her breasts, Laura thought she would explode. And the more he kissed her, the more he touched her, the more she wanted him. She couldn't get enough of him. Judging by his groan when she stroked his manhood, he couldn't get enough of her, either.

He flipped her onto her back, kissed her again. Harder. Deeper. Her tongue matched his, stroke for stroke. Needing to get closer to him still, she pulled at the buttons on his shirt and when his chest was bare, she pressed her mouth to his chest. When she flicked her tongue over his male nipple, she felt his body quiver.

Then his hands were on her again. "I want you naked," he told her and made short work of the buttons on her blouse. He unhooked the front of her bra, bared her breasts. And the look in his eyes sent a shiver through her. "I've dreamed of seeing you like this, of doing this," he said as he lowered his head and took her nipple into his mouth.

Laura gasped. She speared her fingers through his hair. Desperate to have him inside her, she reached for her belt. "Not yet," he whispered as he laved the nipple with his tongue then moved to the other breast and started the process all over again. The sensations were exquisite and maddening. But still he refused to hurry.

While his mouth enjoyed her breasts, he smoothed his hand down her waist, over her hips and beneath her skirt. By the time he slipped his hand inside her panties and cupped her, Laura was quivering with need. When he eased one finger inside her, she could hardly breathe.

He took his time. He stroked the nub of pleasure at her center slowly at first and with each stroke, Laura could feel the need build. She could hear her breathing quickening. He increased the pressure, quickened the pace. And she could feel his own need mounting, hear it with each ragged breath he drew.

"Jack," she cried out as she felt the orgasm building. She pulled his mouth to hers. She kissed him hungrily, greedily, wanting to send him over the edge as he had sent her. Then suddenly the orgasm hit her.

Pulling her mouth free, Laura clutched at his

shoulders. She dug her nails through his shirt and into his skin. Closing her eyes, she tipped her head back and shuddered as she reached the crest and went over. Just when she started to settle, Jack took her up again and again.

But it wasn't enough. Keeping her eyes on his, she reached for him. She heard his breath catch, felt a thrill of power go through her at his reaction to her touch. The feel of the large bulge in his pants sent another wave of desire through her. She fumbled with his belt, got the button of his jeans open. She had just started to ease down his zipper when the elevator jerked to life and they began moving.

Jack didn't know whether to be grateful or seriously ticked off when he realized the elevator was moving and that they were about to be rescued. He'd been moments away from making love with Laura on the floor of the elevator and a part of him was tempted to hit the stop button on the car and finish what they had started.

But then he thought of Laura. Her hair was tumbled and wild-looking. Her eyes were dark and smoky with desire. Her lips were swollen from his kisses and whisker burns were visible on her pale skin. Her skirt was a rumpled mess and she was struggling to button her blouse. She would be mortified for anyone to find them like this, to see her disheveled appearance. And for the first time in a long time, someone else's needs mattered more than his.

"Here," he said, handing her her jacket.

"Thanks," she murmured and slipped it on.

Quickly, Jack buttoned his shirt. When he realized some of the buttons had been broken in her haste to rid him of his shirt, he grabbed his sweater from the floor and pulled it over his head.

Laura had just managed to smooth her hair when the elevator doors opened. And madness ensued.

"Ms. Spencer, are you all right?" the building's maintenance engineer asked.

"What happened?" the housekeeping supervisor asked, concern in her voice.

"I'm fine," Laura said. "The elevator shorted out in the storm."

"Laura, for heaven's sake," Chloe exclaimed as she muscled her way to the front of the elevator and blocked the door. "I was worried sick about you when you didn't come home last night."

"I'm surprised you got home that early," Laura said.

Chloe scowled at her. "Funny."

"What are you doing here at this time of morning, anyway?"

"Looking for you. When you didn't come home and didn't answer your cell or office phones, I was worried. I thought something bad might have happened to you."

"Something bad did happen," Laura replied. "I got stuck in an elevator."

"Is that Mr. Hawke with you?"

"Yes," Jack replied in answer to the hotel bellman's question.

"The front desk has been trying to reach you since last night," he explained. "I think they had an important message for you."

"Thanks. I'll check with them," Jack said.

"What happened to your head?" Chloe asked him.

Jack pressed his fingers against the bandage, but before he could respond, Laura said, "Mr. Hawke tried to get us out of the elevator by climbing up into the elevator shaft, hoping he could reach the next floor through a vent and get help. Unfortunately, the vents were sealed shut. But in the process, he injured himself."

"Pretty brave of you, Jack," Chloe remarked.

"It *was* brave of him," Laura fired back. "But it was also very foolish." She looked at him then, remorse and concern filling her eyes. "We're lucky he didn't fall and seriously injure himself or worse."

"It's just a scratch," Jack replied, more for Laura's benefit than anyone else's.

"You still should see a doctor," she told him.

"I will," he promised. Aware of the curious eyes watching the exchange, Jack wanted to spare Laura any more awkwardness with her staff or her sister, so he cleared a path by saying,

"Now, if you'll excuse us. I think you'll all understand that after spending the night on the floor of a hard, cold elevator, Ms. Spencer and I could both use a hot shower, something to eat and some sleep."

Taking the hint, the people began to disperse—everyone except Chloe, who followed them both to the main lobby. "So you two were stuck in that little old elevator together all night, huh?"

"Yes," Laura said, but Jack noted that she didn't look at her sister. Nor did she look at him. Instead she kept her gaze focused on the floor numbers above the main elevator.

Chloe looked at him and then at her sister. "What did you two do all night?"

"Waited," Laura replied.

Chloe moved a step closer to Laura. "What's that on your face?"

Laura touched her cheek where his whiskers had left their mark. "Nothing. Probably from lying on the floor."

"Doesn't look like a mark from the floor tile

to me." She got even closer. "Looks more like whisker burns. Wonder how they got there?"

Laura flushed and Jack expected her to deny it. Instead, she surprised him by turning to her sister and saying, "Probably the same way you got that hickey on your neck the night you went out with Bobby Connors and his car broke down during your senior year in high school."

"His car did break down," Chloe assured her, color creeping into her cheeks.

"And the elevator did get stuck," Laura countered.

Jack wasn't sure if the argument had continued or not because just as the elevator arrived, the front-desk clerk spotted him. "Mr. Hawke," she called out. "I have your assistant on the line again, sir. She says it's important."

"Tell her I'll be with her in a moment," he told her. Then he turned to Laura, touched her arm. "We need to talk later."

She nodded. "Be sure to have someone take a look at that cut."

"I will," he promised again.

"And when you two finish your 'talk,' don't forget you're supposed to meet with Meredith this afternoon," Chloe reminded him.

Jack didn't miss the knowing look in Laura's sister's eyes. But he didn't shy away from it, either. "I won't forget," he assured her. Once Laura and her sister disappeared into the elevator, Jack headed to the house phone to take Dotty's call, wondering what was so all-fired important.

What was so all-fired important, he soon discovered, was that his stepbrother's father had just initiated a series of stock sales and transfers that, when complete, would net him a cool fifteen million dollars. The exact amount needed to pay off Laura's mother's note, cure the default and stop Jack from foreclosing on the Contessa. Jack had never believed in coincidences. He didn't believe in them now.

Laura didn't believe in omens. She'd never believed that spilling salt, walking beneath a ladder or having a black cat cross your path were signs that something bad was about to happen. But she was beginning to seriously reconsider her decision. After that night she and Jack had spent in the elevator, the main heater in the hotel had died, the sous-chef had quit and a group scheduled to take thirty of the hotel's hundred rooms for a week had canceled due to crippling snowstorms in the north that had shut down the airports. But it was the fact that she had neither seen nor heard from Jack for nearly two days that worried her the most.

When he'd said they needed to talk, she had agreed. While she would have liked nothing better than to go with him up to his suite right then and there, it hadn't been possible. She'd had Chloe itching to hear details, a staff with a million decisions that needed to be made, and she'd been in serious need of food and a bath. But from the way Jack had looked at her, the tender way he had touched her arm, she had been positive he had wanted them to finish what they had started as much as she had.

She still didn't know what the important

business was that had caused him to leave abruptly that morning. Nor did she know why he hadn't told her he was leaving. Had it not been for Chloe mentioning that he'd had to cancel the meeting with Meredith for that afternoon, she wouldn't have known he'd left town. But he was back now. She knew from Alphonse, the doorman, that he had returned late that afternoon. So why hadn't he attempted to see her? They had almost been lovers, for pity's sake.

Lovers.

Just the word sent a thrill through her. She wasn't an innocent young girl. She was a grown woman who had made love before and had enjoyed it. But never, not ever, had she experienced anything close to the pleasure that she had experienced in Jack's arms.

At the mere memory, a ripple of heat swirled through her body. Lifting her hand to her throat, Laura recalled with vivid clarity the feel of his mouth, hot and eager, on her breasts, the feel of his hands, so strong and yet gentle, on her skin. She had no doubt that had it not been for the untimely rescue, they would have made love completely that morning. It was what they both had wanted, what they had been heading toward for weeks now, she admitted.

So why, two full days later, had they still not made love?

Was it possible that she had been mistaken about how much he wanted her? Had those hours they'd spent together really meant nothing to him?

It was imperative she discover the truth. Because somewhere between fighting to stop his takeover of the hotel and lying half-naked in his arms, she had fallen for Jackson Hawke. She'd known him less than a month, had resented the threat he represented to her beloved hotel and she was starting to fall in love with him.

Laura was still digesting the fact that she had feelings for a man who, for all intents and purposes, was her enemy when her cell phone began to ring. Grabbing her purse, she dug into the leather bag and hoped it was Jack. But when she located the phone, she saw her mother's number instead. "Hello, Mother."

"Laura, darling. You'd better sit down."

He was in a foul mood, Jack admitted as he walked over to the window and looked out over the city. Night had fallen. On the streets below he could see people scampering, their arms most probably laden with shopping bags and wrapped packages. Everywhere he'd turned over the past two days, people were in a cheerful, holiday mood.

Not him.

He was angry, Jack acknowledged. He was angry with Matt Peterson. He was angry with Laura for lying to him. But most of all, he was angry with himself. He'd allowed himself to become distracted. He'd allowed his emotions to interfere with business. He'd allowed his attraction to Laura to distract him. And because he had, he was on the verge of blowing a fifteen-million-dollar deal.

Peterson was going to bail her out. Unless Jack found a way to foreclose before Peterson could get his funds in place, his deal was dead and Laura would keep the hotel. And Peterson would keep Laura. He didn't like losing. But he'd lost deals before and probably would again in the future. He wouldn't have even minded losing to Laura and seeing her win their bet. What he did mind was losing to his stepbrother. Losing *Laura* to him.

He didn't want her to matter. He didn't want to care about her. But it was because he did care for her that he hated like hell to see her with someone like Peterson. She deserved better than his stepbrother. Hell, she deserved someone better than *him*.

Caught up in his musing, it took Jack a moment to register that the pounding he heard was coming from the door. Turning away from the window, he strode through the suite and opened the door to Laura.

He knew instantly that something was wrong. Her eyes had a wild look to them. Her dark red hair, a tangled mass around her face and shoulders, looked as though she'd been running in the wind.

Her eyes were dry, but there were tear streaks down her cheeks. "What's wrong?" he demanded.

"I guess that depends on who you ask," she told him and pushed past him into the suite.

Jack closed the door and followed her. "Since you're the one who came barging into my suite, I'm asking you. What are you doing here?"

"I'm here to pay off on our bet," she told him and stepped out of her heels.

Jack narrowed his eyes. Keeping his voice even, he said, "You're a little early. You've still got another five days."

"Five days or five months. It won't matter," she informed him. "My mother came up two million short in the refinancing. You've won, Hawke," she said, her voice cracking. "The Contessa is yours and I'm here to deliver on my end of the deal."

What was she talking about? Didn't she know Peterson was going to give her the money? But if she knew, she wouldn't be there. She would be with Peterson. "As much as I'd like to collect on our bet," he began with a casualness he didn't feel, "you might want to hold off. The rest of the money could still turn up."

"It won't. And I want to pay off now."

"Laura, you don't have to do this," he told her. "You don't want to do this."

"Sure I do." She pulled her sweater over her head. "We had a bet and I lost. I'm here to pay off the debt."

Jack's mouth went dry at the sight of her in the black lace bra. He was rock hard in an instant. Fighting the desire clawing at his gut, he told himself he shouldn't do this. He would not do this. He would not take advantage of her when it was obvious that she was upset and apparently didn't realize that Peterson was going to come through for her. When they'd started this thing, there had been a part of him that had wanted to bed her, had deliberately planned to do just that, to get back at his stepbrother. But that had changed and he knew he could never use her that way. He refused to do so now. Snatching up her sweater from the floor, he threw it at her and walked over to open the door of the suite. "Go home, Laura," he said through a voice that had gone hoarse with need.

He didn't expect the flash of anger in her eyes. She threw his sweater back on the floor and followed him across the room where she slammed the door shut. Then she turned to look at him. Taking his face in both of her hands, she kissed his mouth. When he didn't respond, she ran her tongue across his lips. Lifting her head, she looked up at him and said, "I'm not going anywhere, Hawke. Not until I've paid off my debt."

His body trembled with need. He wanted to haul her into the bedroom and make love to her until neither of them could remember their names. He wanted to feel her body shudder and clench around him when he filled her. He wanted to hear her call his name and cling to him as he took them both over the edge.

But he didn't.

He couldn't.

Not now. Not when she was so vulnerable, when she was still reeling because she thought she'd lost her hotel. Not when he knew that his stepbrother was going to bail her out even if she did not. He couldn't make love to her with the lie between them. If he did, she would hate him. And the idea that Laura would look at him with disgust and hatred hurt far worse than he ever imagined it would.

With a strength he hadn't known he possessed, Jack caught her hands and ended the kiss. "I was never serious about the bet. It was just a joke," he lied. "Go home, Laura. Before you embarrass us both."

He braced himself, sure he would see shock and hurt in her eyes. Instead he looked into the green eyes of a siren. "So you're saying you don't want me?"

"That's right."

The smile that curved her lips was pure sin. She stepped into his space, stroked his arousal through his slacks. "Liar."

Jack groaned. Unable to resist her, he pulled her into his arms and kissed her with all the hunger, all the need that had been building inside him from the first time he'd laid eyes on her. Tonight, he told himself, tonight she was his. Lifting her in his arms, he carried her into the bedroom.

Ten

Laura could feel the coolness of the silk sheets on her heated skin as Jack placed her on the bed. The contrast served to sober her for a moment. She'd come to him in a frenzy of despair and hurt following her mother's phone call. Those feelings had soon given way to anger. Anger at herself, her mother, her grandfather for not trusting her with his hotel. And anger at Jack for taking the hotel. At Jack for making her love him and then turning away. So she'd come to him. One look into those cool blue eyes and she'd known he was shutting her out. She didn't know why he had turned away from her. She didn't understand why he would deny what was between them. She only knew that she needed him to feel as she was feeling.

He stood beside the bed looking down at her. He wanted her. She could see it in his eyes, etched in the rigid way he held his body. But she could also see he was struggling with the decision to make love with her as he wanted, as they both wanted.

Determined not to let him deny them both, she took his hand and brought it to her breast, held it there. Desire flared in his blue eyes as he squeezed her sensitive flesh through her bra. "Make love with me, Jack," she whispered.

"Laura, you don't need to do this."

"Yes, I do. I want you, Jack. And I know you want me."

This time he didn't deny it. And when she reached for him, he came to her. The feel of his body against hers drove all thoughts away save for the feel of him, the taste of him, the ache at her center that grew stronger with each stroke of his tongue. In a frenzy to be one with him, Laura reached for his zipper.

He tore his mouth free and captured her fingers. "No," he told her. "I'm not going to let you rush this. I'm going to make love to you slowly and enjoy every inch of you. And when I finish, I'm going to start all over again. I want you to remember tonight, Laura. I want you to remember me."

She started to tell him that she doubted she would be able to forget him if she tried, but then he was kissing her again and she forgot what she wanted to say. All she knew was that her body was taut with need and awash with sensation as Jack moved his mouth from her lips to her jaw. From there he worked his way down her neck to her shoulder. He veered left and without removing her bra, he closed his mouth over the tip of her breast. When his teeth closed around her nipple, Laura nearly came off the bed at the exquisite sensations that rolled through her.

He unhooked her bra, bared her breasts and took them in his hands. Laura moaned as he kneaded and kissed and plucked at her nipples. Then his clever mouth kissed a path down her rib cage to her belly. Her stomach quivered as his tongue circled her navel. By the time he pulled off her skirt and panties, tossing them aside, Laura was frantic to feel him inside her. She reached for him, fought with the buckle of his belt. "You're wearing too many clothes," she complained.

Between them, they made short work of his shirt and slacks. His groan as she freed him from his briefs sent a thrill of excitement through her. But excitement turned to white-hot need as he moved down her body and parted her thighs. "Jack, no."

"Yes." Opening her, he kissed her.

The first stroke of his tongue sent an explosion of sensation through her. When he repeated the process, she gasped. He continued to kiss her, to taste her, to nip her with his teeth. And with each flick of his tongue she could feel the pressure building. Just when she thought she couldn't stand the pleasure another second he increased the pressure and Laura felt the world explode.

"Jack," she cried out, reaching for him.

Then he was inside her. One smooth, slow stroke after the other, moving in and out. In and out. Nearly withdrawing, then filling her again. Then he started to move faster and faster still as he pushed her, pushed them closer and closer to that precipice.

"Look at me, Laura," he commanded.

She looked at him, stared into eyes that had gone dark with need. And desperation. She wondered at the desperation, wanted to ask him what was wrong. Then he entered her again, and the room around her shifted, shattered. And then she was tumbling into space.

Wave after wave shuddered through her, stealing her breath, stealing her ability to think. All she could do was feel. When the orgasm ripped through Jack, it sent her free-falling again. Driving into her one last time, he cried out her name. As his body convulsed, she held on to him, felt each spasm as it hit him before it rolled into her. Finally, when the shudders stopped, they continued to cling to one another.

For a long time, she said nothing. Neither did he. She contented herself with the feel of his body next to hers, the strength of his arms wrapped around her. She didn't allow herself to think beyond the moment. She didn't know where they went from here, if they went anywhere at all. Jack had made no promises. Neither had she. But she knew in her heart that it was promises she wanted.

"We need to talk, Laura. There's something I need to tell you about the foreclosure. You—"

"I don't want to talk about business," she told him. Turning over, she faced him. "What happened between us just now wasn't business."

"But—"

"It was personal, Jack. And I didn't come here tonight to try to convince you not to foreclose on the hotel. I came here tonight because I wanted to be with you. I wanted you. I needed you."

"But there's something I need to tell you. Something you need to know about me," he began.

Laura pressed her finger to his lips. "I know everything I need to know about you. I know that you're smart and arrogant and a tough business-man. I know you can be ruthless, but that you're brave and more caring than you want anyone to know. I know you're a wonderful and generous lover," she said softly as she stroked his jaw.

"I was inspired," he told her, then captured her hand and placed a kiss in her palm.

As impossible as it seemed, she could feel desire curling in her belly again. With a boldness she would never have imagined she possessed, she said, "Maybe I can inspire you again."

Heat flared in his eyes, but his expression grew somber. "You inspire me just by breathing. But you may feel differently when you know the truth about me, about who I am."

"I know who you are, Jackson Hawke. You're the man I'm in love with." When he went still, Laura quickly added, "I didn't tell you how I feel because I expect a declaration from you. I don't. But I wanted you to know the way I feel. I love you."

"Laura, if you knew the truth—"

"The only truth that matters to me right now is that you want me. Do you want me, Jack?"

"Yes," he said, his voice gruff. "I want you… more than I've ever wanted anything or anyone in my life."

"Then show me," she told him.

Jack showed her over and over again throughout the night. With his mouth. With his hands. With his body. And when she awoke in the morning, feeling tender and achy from their lovemaking, he lifted her in his arms and carried her into the bathroom. In the shower, he soaped her body, bathed every inch of her, discovered new pleasure points she hadn't known existed.

"You're so beautiful," he murmured. "So soft," he told her as he worked his way up from her feet to her thighs and the sensitive spot between them. With a slowness that she found maddening, he finally reached her breasts. Then his mouth was on hers, pressing her against the wall while the shower poured over them.

He lifted her onto him and she wrapped her legs around his waist and then he began to move. With each thrust, Laura could feel herself moving closer and closer to the edge of the cliff.

And with the water streaming down around their joined bodies, she felt herself begin to fall,

"Jack," she called out, clutching his shoulders as the sensations took her over that cliff.

Moments later, she heard him shout her name as he followed her over the edge.

By the time she exited the bedroom forty-five minutes later, Jack was already dressed in a suit and tie, sitting at the table talking on his cell phone. She noted his briefcase and laptop sat near the door.

"I know it's last-minute, Dotty. But try to set the meeting up with as many of them as you can. If they can't make it, get them to agree to be available for a teleconference." He paused. "Just tell them it's a one-time chance for them to make a thirty percent return on their investment, but I need an answer by tomorrow."

For the first time since she'd shown up at his hotel room door the previous night, Laura felt awkward. They were lovers and she loved him, but she didn't know how he felt. Had last night been a one-time fling for him? Would he want to continue to see her? Or would he foreclose on the hotel and return to New York and never see her again? A sinking feeling settled in her stomach as she realized she didn't have the answers and that those answers may very well not be what she wanted. It also reminded her that Jack had wanted to tell her something last night. Only she had been fearful that whatever he wanted to tell her would ruin what was happening between them, so she had refused. Now in the clear light of day, she realized that might not have been the smartest thing to do.

As though sensing her presence, Jack looked up. "I've got to go, Dotty. I'll see you in a couple of hours." Ending the call, he went to Laura and kissed her. When he lifted his head, he smiled and said, "Good morning, again."

"Good morning."

"I ordered some coffee, croissants, eggs and bacon from room service," he told her and Laura noted for the first time the serving cart piled with silver trays. "I wasn't sure what you liked to eat in the morning."

"Just coffee for now," she said and sat down while he retrieved the silver pot. "Are you going somewhere?"

"I have to go to New York this morning," he told her as he poured her a cup of coffee.

"I see," she said, but she clearly didn't. "Will you be coming back?"

He stopped in the middle of pouring his own coffee at the question. "Of course I'll be back. Why would you think I wouldn't?"

Both relieved and somewhat embarrassed, she said, "I just wasn't sure. I mean, I was the one who showed up here last night and refused to take no for an answer."

He caught her hands, pulled her to her feet. "And I'm glad you did. I meant what I said last night. I've never wanted anything or anyone as much as I wanted you. As much as I *still* want you," he added.

Laura went into his arms, laid her head against his chest. As she breathed in his scent, reveled in the feel of him, she asked, "Do you really have to go to New York now?"

Taking her by the shoulders, he gently set her from him. "I'd like nothing better than to take you into that bedroom and make love to you again. But there's something I have to do first, something I have to fix. Once I've made things right, I'll be back."

"How long will you be gone?"

"A day, maybe two tops. And when I get back, we'll talk."

"About the foreclosure," she said, realizing he would be back right before the scheduled fore-closure on the hotel.

"Yes, we'll talk about that. And about us."

It took a lot longer to fix his situation than he'd anticipated, Jack admitted as he sat across the table the next afternoon with the signed documents in hand. It had also cost him an additional million dollars to sweeten an already very sweet deal. But he'd done it. The foreclosure on the Contessa Hotel by Hawke Industries was now officially canceled. In turn, the investors he'd originally sold the idea to were

enjoying a hefty return for their initial investment. And he was now the sole owner of the
promissory note and the foreclosure was called
off. The entire process had been tricky at best
and he'd had to tiptoe around the legality of his
actions because of the potential conflict of
interest. Fortunately, the attorneys had ham-
mered it out.

Standing at the door, Jack shook hands with
each investor and bade them goodbye. "Thanks
again, Carlton," Jack said.

"Anytime, Hawke," the other man said and
shook his hand. "You call me again the next time
you're willing to offer these kind of terms on a
deal."

"Me, too," one of Carlton's cronies said with
a laugh.

Everyone left but his final investor and his
father's old friend, Tom Ryan. "Thanks for
coming, Tom."

He nodded. "You know, son, I've known you
since you were knee high. I watched you go
through your parents' nasty divorce and your

father's bout with the bottle. I watched you grow into a fine young man, but a hard one, a man who never allowed himself to feel anything deeply or look at anything beyond the bottom line. For you, everything has always come down to money. I suspect a lot of that had to do with what happened with your parents. And I understood it, but I worried about you."

"Is there a point here somewhere, Tom?" Jack asked, not particularly happy with the portrait he'd heard painted of himself.

"The point is that today you made a business decision that I suspect had nothing to do with the bottom line. Unless I miss my guess, you just blew several million dollars for personal reasons."

Which was true, Jack admitted silently. Feeling somewhat defensive, he said, "What if I did? You and the others certainly profited from it."

Tom smiled, his brown eyes twinkling. "Yes, we did. And I wasn't being critical, son. Hell, I'm pleased about it because I was worried you were going to end up a rich but lonely man."

And he just might have, Jack realized. Had it not been for Laura. Laura had changed all that. Laura had changed him. "Glad I could make you happy," Jack said. "But if you don't mind, I've got a plane to catch."

"Just one more thing, Jack. Tell me. Was she worth it?"

Jack smiled for the first time since he'd left New Orleans two days ago. "Yeah, she was."

And as he dashed from his office to the waiting limo for the airport, all Jack could think about was that Laura had been worth not only the millions it had cost him on this deal, but she had been worth everything he had and more. Now all he had to do was hope that she would forgive him for not telling her right from the start that Matt Peterson was his stepbrother and convince her that a future with him was worth the risk.

"Thank you. Yes, I'll get back to you about the date for the press conference," Laura said then hung up the phone with the business office at City Park.

Jack. Jack had done this for her.

Picking up the letter from the park's Celebration in the Oaks Improvement Committee, she reread the words of thanks for the donation to restore the Carousel House. She skimmed the remainder of the letter, asking her to confirm the wording on the commemorative plaque that would grace the Carousel House in her grandfather's name. Her heart swelled. Jack had made the donation before their night together. Surely for him to do such a thing had to mean he felt something more for her than lust, she told herself.

She thought of his phone call earlier, telling her he was on his way back and would meet her at her house. He'd said he had something to tell her. Was this what he'd wanted to tell her earlier? Then she'd let him surprise her and after he did, she would show him just how much she appreciated what he'd done.

"That's an awfully dreamy expression for a woman who's supposedly working. Don't you agree, Meredith?"

Laura opened her eyes and looked over at the doorway where her sister stood with Meredith Grant. The daughter of a Boston blue blood and an opera diva, Meredith had been Chloe's step-sister during the brief marriage of Chloe's father and Meredith's mother. As in Laura's own case, divorce had not severed the family bonds. Laura smiled at the two of them.

"I think she looks like a woman who's working at dreaming up some wonderful new marketing plan for her hotel," Meredith offered diplomatically, a hint of her Boston roots in her voice.

"Thank you, Meredith," she said and couldn't help but notice the contrast in the two women. While her sister, Chloe, was striking, in-your-face sexy and fun, Meredith was a quiet beauty with an abundance of grace and poise. And where her sister's style was up-to-the-minute chic and bold, Meredith's was elegant.

"You're quite welcome," Meredith told her politely.

"So what are you two doing here? I thought Chloe was dragging you off to some party tonight."

"Not some party," Chloe corrected. "It's a party being hosted by the director of the new action/adventure movie they're planning to shoot here. Oops," Chloe said as her cell phone started to ring. She glanced at the number. "I need to take this," she told them and exited the office.

"Your sister seems to think there could be a few potential clients for me among the Hollywood South set," Meredith explained, referring to the name many were now calling New Orleans's fast-growing movie industry. "Laura, I hope you don't mind, but Chloe told me about your situation with the hotel. I have some money in a trust fund I could borrow against and lend you if it would help."

Moved by the gesture, Laura reached out and squeezed the other woman's hand. "I can't tell you how much I appreciate the offer, Meredith. But I can't accept. I've pretty much resigned myself to the fact that come Monday, Hawke Industries will be the majority owner of the Contessa."

"I'm sorry," Meredith told her.

"So am I." She sighed. "But I guess the one good thing that's come out of all this is that I met Jack."

"Oh. I didn't realize the two of you were… involved."

Laura frowned, not sure what to make of Meredith's reaction. "Is there any reason I shouldn't be involved with Jack?" When the other woman remained silent, Laura pressed, "Please, Meredith, if there's something you think I should know, tell me."

The clear blue eyes that looked at her were filled with concern and empathy. "It's just that…in my business I try to keep up with the society columns and based on what I'd read and things Chloe said a while back, I was under the impression that you were involved with Matthew Peterson. In fact, I thought it was rather serious."

"Matt and I did date for a while," she confessed. "And for a short time, I thought it might become more serious. But when I moved back to New Orleans, we agreed to take a bit of a break. We have sort of had a long-distance relationship since then. But it isn't serious. At least not anymore," she told her, which was something she realized she still needed to make clear to Matt. Now with Jack in her life, she could see even more clearly that what she shared with Matt was not real love and to allow him to believe otherwise would not be fair.

"Does Jackson Hawke know that? I mean, does he know that you and Matthew Peterson are no longer a couple?"

"I'm not sure. But then I'm not sure he ever knew Matt and I were involved in the first place. Why? What difference does it make?"

Meredith clasped her hands in that way well-bred women do when they need to compose themselves. When she looked up at Laura, her gaze was steady and her voice gentle as she said, "It might make a difference because Matthew Peterson and Jackson Hawke are stepbrothers."

The news hit Laura like a blow.

"You didn't know." It was a statement, not a question.

"No, I didn't."

"I guess it's not surprising that he didn't tell you," Meredith said. "From what I'm told there's a lot of bad blood between the two of them. It goes back to when Hawke's mother left him and his father for Matt Peterson's dad. I understand Matt Peterson doesn't even acknowledge there's any family connection between the two of them, even though it was Hawke's mother who adopted Peterson. And before you think I'm some terrible gossip, the only reason I know all this is because my mother is friends with Nicole Peterson. She performed at some charity event Mrs. Peterson was chairing."

"I don't think you're a gossip at all," Laura assured her. "Is there… Is there anything else I should know?"

Again, Meredith hesitated. "Just that the rivalry between Jackson Hawke and his step-brother has only gotten worse as they've gotten older. In fact, when I was having such a difficult time getting an appointment with Hawke to discuss my business proposal, my assistant went so far as to suggest I approach Matt Peterson with the proposal because the chance to snatch a deal from his stepbrother would be a sure way to draw Hawke's interest. I'm ashamed to say I actually considered it."

"No one would have blamed you, if you had," Laura said absently.

"I would have blamed me. That's not how I do business," Meredith explained. Then her expression softened again. "I'm so sorry, Laura."

"Me, too. I just still can't believe that Jack didn't tell me he and Matt are stepbrothers."

"Maybe he didn't know about you and Matt Peterson," Meredith offered. "I mean, I read the gossip and society sections because of my business. It's possible Hawke doesn't pay any attention to them and never realized you had been involved with his stepbrother."

Had Jack known about her involvement with Matt? Of course he would have known. He'd had her investigated. Her personal relationships, particularly a long one with a wealthy and well-connected businessman would have been noted. Suddenly memories came flooding back—of the night in her office when Matt had called and Jack

had left abruptly in a surly mood. She also remembered his odd remark about what would
Peterson say when he called for her and she
wasn't home. Yes, Jack had known about her relationship with Matt. What she didn't know was
if Jack had really wanted her, or had he only
wanted what he thought belonged to Matt?

As though sensing her turmoil, Meredith said,
"Laura, if he did know about you and his stepbrother and didn't say anything, he might have
had a good reason."

"Can you think of a good reason?" she asked.

"No, but if I were you, I would talk to him and
find out what his reasons were."

"I intend to," Laura told her. And she prayed
that when she did talk to Jack, the answers he
gave her wouldn't break her heart.

"Good luck, then."

"Thanks," she said. "And thanks for being
honest with me. I know I put you on the spot."

"I just hope that when you talk to Hawke that
you get the answers you want."

"So do I," Laura said.

Eleven

Jack spied the flashing police car lights behind him and breathed a relieved sigh when the officer whizzed past him. He had no doubt he'd broken several speeding laws in his race from the airport to Laura's house. Reminding himself to send a donation to the policemen's fund as atonement and thanks, he exited Interstate 10. As he waited for the light to change, he turned on the radio and found himself listening to the Christmas carol about being home for Christmas. Jack smiled, realizing that in a manner of speaking he was coming home—to the first home he'd had in a very long time. And for the first time in even longer, he was actually looking forward to Christmas.

Because of Laura.

His heart seemed to swell in his chest as he thought of her, remembered the feel of her, the scent of her, the sound of her telling him she loved him. He wanted to see her face, hold her close and hear her say those words to him again. And she would, he told himself. Once he told her that the foreclosure on the Contessa had been canceled, it would no longer stand between them. She would no longer need to worry about losing her beloved hotel and he would no longer have to worry about Peterson injecting himself into Laura's life.

Later, he would tell her about Peterson, explain their connection and hope she would forgive him for not telling her about it earlier. But no matter what happened, she would never know that he had even considered seducing her to get back at his stepbrother. That he had thought of doing so still shamed him. He could live with his shame, but he couldn't live with the hurt that it would cause Laura. Whatever it took, he would keep that truth from her.

Deep in thought and eager to see Laura, Jack didn't even see the man standing on the stairs in front of her house until after he had parked and exited the car. Even though his back was to him, Jack recognized the tall figure in the black overcoat sporting his two-hundred-dollar haircut. Jack also recognized the voice talking on the cell phone.

"Laura, it's Matt again. I've got a surprise for you, babe. Give me a call."

Jealousy and anger gripped Jack by the throat and refused to let go. He balled his hands into fists. And when Peterson turned around, he didn't look at all surprised to see Jack there.

"Hello, Hawke."

"What are you doing here?" Jack demanded.

"I could ask you the same thing. This is Laura's apartment, after all. And she is *my* girlfriend. Not yours."

"She might have been your girlfriend at one time, but she's not anymore," Jack told him.

"Are you sure about that?" Peterson asked. He leaned back against the door, a smug look on his face. "Laura and I have been seeing each other for more than a year. In fact, Mom and Dad adore her and they're eager to welcome her into our family."

The mention of his mother and the insinuation that Laura would be marrying Matt infuriated Jack. But he forced himself not to give in to Peterson's baiting. It had been a mistake he'd made far too often in their youth. As a result, he'd ended up being the one getting the bad rap and Peterson had come out smelling like a rose. "Give it up, Peterson. Laura's done with you."

"I don't think so."

Jack couldn't help noticing that his stepbrother had made the statement with the same confidence he'd possessed as an eight-year-old when he'd told Jack that his mother wouldn't be coming back for him. Peterson had been right. His mother hadn't come back for him. She had started a new life with a new son. But Peterson wasn't right this time, Jack told himself.

When he didn't respond to the provoking,

Peterson continued, "As a matter of fact, I'm so sure about Laura that I'm planning to announce our engagement at Christmas. She'll make the perfect candidate's wife, don't you think?" He paused. "After all, she is the whole package. Smart, beautiful and of course, there's that sexy little body of hers."

"Shut up," Jack warned.

Peterson smiled, his lips twisting malevolently. He was clearly enjoying himself. "What do you think she's going to say when I give her the check to pay off her mother's loan and stop you from foreclosing on that hotel that she loves so much? I've got it right here," he said, patting his pocket. "I imagine she's going to be very grateful and I certainly am looking forward to letting her show me her appreciation."

Jack wanted to plant his fist in Matt's face. Instead, he took a step forward. "I said to shut up!"

"Why? Don't like the idea of Laura showing me her gratitude with that sweet little body of hers?"

"Don't hold your breath, Peterson. She isn't going to show you anything but the door because the foreclosure was canceled. I bought out the other investors. So you see, Laura doesn't need your money or you. Now why don't you go hop on the plane and go back home to mommy and daddy."

Peterson laughed and the sound did nothing to ease Jack's temper. "Come on, Hawke. Do you honestly believe that given a choice Laura would choose you over me? Face it, you're a loser. Just like your old man was."

Jack wasn't sure if it was hearing Peterson tag him as a loser again or if was the seed of uncertainty that Laura might indeed choose his stepbrother over him, but something inside of him snapped. Grabbing Peterson by the lapels of his coat, Jack hauled him up to get right in his face and said, "Since it's my bed Laura's been sleeping in and my name she screams when I'm buried inside her, I'd say you're the loser this time. Not me."

At the sound of a gasp behind him, Jack spun around and saw Laura standing there on the sidewalk. In the streetlight, her face was the color of chalk and her green eyes were the size of quarters. But it was the look in those eyes, the shock, the hurt, that ripped at him now. Releasing Peterson, he started down the steps toward her. "Laura—"

"Don't," she said, holding up her hand.

"I can explain," he told her, desperate to wipe that shattered expression off her face. "It's not what it looks like."

"Isn't it?" she asked, her voice flat, cold.

"No," he told her firmly. "It's not."

"Don't listen to him, Laura," Matt said as he straightened his coat. "It's exactly what it looks like. Hawke has hated me from the day his mother left his old man and him to be with me and my father. He's always been jealous that his mother chose us over him and what he hated most was that I was the son she really loved, not him. He'd do anything to get back at me for that."

"Including using me," Laura remarked, but her eyes remained fixed on Jack.

"No," he told her.

"That's exactly what he did. It's all a game to

him," Matt assured her. "He found out about us, knew that I was in love with you and he devised this elaborate scheme to try to hurt me by taking you from me. Why do you think he bought your mother's note? He knew the threat of foreclosing on the hotel would make you vulnerable to him. He even went to the trouble of getting the foreclosure canceled just so he could play hero and make you indebted to him."

"And what about you, Matt? Why are you here? To play white knight for me, so that I'll be grateful to you?"

"Babe, I'm here because I love you. I knew something was wrong the last time we talked. As soon as I found out what was going on here I knew that Hawke had to be involved. And I'll admit, I did get the money you needed but that's because I know how much that old hotel means to you."

"Or maybe you got the money so that I would be indebted to you instead," she countered and there was no mistaking the cynicism in her voice.

"I did it so that you would see how much you mean to me. I want a lifetime with you, Laura, not a few nights of cheap sex. Because that's all it was to him," Peterson told her. "You heard him yourself. He bragged to me that he'd slept with you just to get even with me."

"That's a lie," Jack insisted.

"Is it, Jack?" Laura asked. "Did you know about me and Matt?"

"Yes, but—"

"Don't listen to any more of his lies, Laura," Peterson told her. He came down off the steps, stood before her and reached for her hands. And the sight of Peterson touching her was like a knife in Jack's heart.

"I love you," Jack told her, saying the words he'd never said to anyone since he was a six-year-old boy, pleading with his mother not to leave him. "And that's not a lie. It's the truth. I may not have been honest about anything else, but that much is the truth. I love you."

"I'm afraid that's not enough," she told him and pulled her hands free from Peterson. "Now if you'll both get out of my way, I'd like to go inside my house."

"Laura, please let me explain," Jack said as she brushed past him and climbed the stairs.

"It's a little late for explanations," she told him. "You'll have my letter of resignation in the morning."

"What about your staff?" he asked, hoping her loyalty and concern for her employees would persuade her to reconsider and give him time to somehow convince her that he hadn't meant to hurt her, that he loved her.

"I'll draft a statement and speak with them individually. But under the circumstances, I won't be giving the customary two weeks' notice because I'll be leaving town." She unlocked the door, paused and turned. "Oh, and if you still want to buy my stock, Jack, it's yours."

"You've made the right decision, Laura," Peterson told her, triumph in his eyes as he started to follow her. "We'll go back to California and put this whole ugly thing behind us."

Laura blocked him at the door. "You'll go back to California, Matt. You and I are done."

"You can't mean that," he countered.

"Oh, but I do mean it. I'm not in love with you, Matt. I don't think I ever was. So I guess you were right, Jack. Matt is the loser this time. But so are you. Because I loved you, but I'll never forgive you for what you've done."

"Come on, Laura. It's Meredith's last night here. You have to come with us," Chloe all but whined as she followed her out of the house to her car.

Laura loaded the empty cardboard boxes into her trunk and closed it. "I told you, I have too much to do. I've got to clear out my desk, make a list of personal items at the hotel that belong to the family, draft a statement for the employees and update my résumé. I don't have time to go to the Celebration in the Oaks. You and Meredith will just have to go without me."

Besides, Laura thought as she walked around to the front of the car and unlocked the driver's-side door, she didn't know if she could face seeing the lights in the oaks with the memory of her evening there with Jack still so fresh in her mind. She'd spent the remainder of Friday evening and the better part of Saturday alternately crying and cursing Jackson Hawke. But nothing she had done had assuaged the ache in her heart over what he'd done.

"But it's Christmas," Chloe continued, refusing to give up. "This will be my first time going to see the lights since Granddad died. And who knows, it might be my last time to see it. And it might be yours, too, if you insist on selling your shares of the Contessa to Jack and leaving New Orleans."

Her sister was right. She didn't know if she would come back again. With her grandfather gone and the Contessa belonging to Jack now, there seemed little reason for her to return to New Orleans. The realization sent another swirl of sorrow through her. New Orleans had always been the one place to which she'd returned. It was her anchor. It was her home.

"Oh, do come," Meredith urged in that perfect diction that Laura found so lovely. "I've heard so much about this Celebration in the Oaks and the antique carousel. I can't wait to see it and Chloe tells me you're a fountain of information about it."

Feeling as though she were being double-teamed, she said, "I'd hardly call the few facts and figures I know a fountain. And as much as I'd like to go, I really am too busy."

"Don't you want to see the Carousel House one last time? Say goodbye to Pegasus?" Chloe asked.

"Pegasus?" Meredith repeated.

"Her favorite horse on the carousel," Chloe explained.

But mention of the horse brought tears to Laura's eyes. She thought of her visits to the Carousel Gardens with her grandfather, the young dreams and fantasies she'd spun while riding on that horse. She thought of telling Jack about those dreams and fantasies, of the tender way he had looked at her while he'd listened, of that first time he'd kissed her under the trees in view of the carousel. Then she thought of the donation he'd made in her grandfather's name to restore the antique ride. An act of love, she had thought at the time. Only she had been wrong. Instead of an act of love, it had merely been part of his great plan to seduce her as a means of revenge against his stepbrother.

Evidently taking her silence as refusal, her sister decided to change her tactics and said, "It's because of Jack, isn't it? He's the real reason you won't come with us."

"He's part of it," Laura admitted. A big part, she added silently.

Chloe planted her hands on her hips, flattened her lips in a disapproving line. "I get that you love him and he hurt you. I even get that you're willing to let him take the Contessa from you and leave town because of what he did. What I don't get is why you would let him steal all the good memories you have of that carousel and the Christmas lights in the oaks."

"I'm not."

"Aren't you? I know how special that old carousel is to you, how much you looked forward to going to see it and the lights each Christmas. It's all you talked about from the moment you saw October on the calendar. You couldn't wait to come home to see the lights and ride your horse on the carousel. But you won't even go now to take a look at it and share it with me or Meredith and it's because you went there with Jack." She paused. "He stole your heart and broke it, Laura. Don't let him steal all your precious memories, too. Say you'll come with me and Meredith tonight."

"All right. I'll come with you," Laura said.

Chloe all but beamed and Laura didn't miss the satisfied smile she sent Meredith's way. "Great."

"You won't be sorry, Laura," Meredith told her. "Tonight you'll make a new memory, a happy memory."

Although she thought the remark odd, Laura shrugged it off. "I'm not going to be making any memories at all if you two don't let me get out of here so I can get to the office and pack."

Both stepped back from the car while Laura got in behind the wheel. "The gates open at dark, which will be around five, but I'll probably be lucky to be finished before six.

Why don't I just meet you guys there for around seven," she suggested.

Chloe's smile faded. "But I thought we'd all go together and get there when it opens."

Laura considered all she had to do and the already late hour. She didn't want to let clearing out her office drag on to the next day. Her plan was to go into the office in the morning, speak with Penny and a few of the other longtime employees before making her announcement and leaving.

"Won't it be especially crowded if we wait that late?" Meredith asked.

Meredith was right. On the weekend before Christmas, attendance was highest. "The best I can do is six-thirty," Laura said.

"Six," Chloe insisted. "Six-thirty is when all the people who went to early dinner will be stopping to tour the lights."

"All right. Six o'clock," Laura relented.

"And we'll pick you up at the hotel," Meredith informed her. At Laura's querying look, the other woman simply explained, "I understand parking is a problem. Best to not have to worry about two cars."

"All right. I'll see you at six."

By the time six o'clock rolled around, Laura was emotionally and physically exhausted. After loading the boxes into her car, she returned to the office for one final look. She had known that packing up her office would be difficult. She had also known that packing away family mementos like the photos of her grandfather and great-grandfather would be bittersweet. She had even known that losing the Contessa would hurt. She had had so many dreams about running the hotel, continuing her grandfather's legacy. What she hadn't known was that losing her dream of a future with Jack would hurt even more.

It wasn't meant to be, she told herself and sighed. She looked around the office, ran her fingertips across the old mahogany desk one final time, then she shut the door and went downstairs to meet her sister and Meredith.

When Laura exited the hotel, she wasn't surprised to see a limo parked out front. Limos were as common as taxis it seemed. What did surprise her was Alphonse, the doorman, informing her that the limo was for her. Wary, Laura approached the sleek black vehicle and when the driver opened the back door, she was equally surprised to see her sister and Meredith. Chloe was dressed in an eye-catching red leather skirt and boots and Meredith in chic mocha-colored suede slacks with matching jacket. But it was the red Santa hats, champagne glasses and the ear-to-ear grins that caused her to do a double take. "What's going on?" she asked.

"Hurry and get in," Chloe insisted. "You're letting all the cold air inside."

Laura climbed into the backseat. "All right, what's with the limo? Did you to hit the jackpot at Harrah's?" she asked, referring to the city's only land-based casino.

"Actually, we're celebrating," Chloe said and poured her a glass of champagne.

Laura took the glass, but didn't drink. "Just what is it we're celebrating?"

"I landed a contract with Hawke Industries yesterday to act as a matchmaker between businesses," Meredith told her.

"That's wonderful, Meredith. Why didn't you say something earlier?" Laura asked. "We should have celebrated last night."

"Given the situation with you and Jack…Mr. Hawke," she amended, "I didn't feel it was appropriate. But Chloe insisted I tell you. She said you would be happy for me and want to celebrate my success."

"She was right. I am happy for you," Laura told her honestly. "Just because things didn't work out for me and Jack personally is no reason for you to pass up a good business opportunity. I wish you every success," she added, clinking her glass with theirs in a toast.

"He was quite remarkable, you know," Meredith told her. "He had some wonderful ideas, ones I had never even thought of."

"I'm not surprised. He's a brilliant businessman," Laura remarked.

While Meredith and Chloe chatted, Laura fell

silent. She stared out the window of the limo, but her thoughts remained filled with Jack. She had half expected to see him at the hotel when she'd gone to pack. If she were honest, a part of her had even hoped she might see him. The truth was now that the initial shock and hurt had subsided some, she wanted to believe that he hadn't meant those things he'd said to Matt, that he hadn't used her. She wanted to believe that what they had shared hadn't all been a lie.

She'd refused to speak with him when he'd tried to talk to her that night. She had ignored each of his calls and not even Chloe's urging her to speak with him had made her relent. But she'd known he'd been outside her apartment most of the night. Between bouts of crying and anger, she'd looked out the window and seen him standing there next to his car. With his arms folded, seemingly oblivious to the bone-chilling cold that was part of New Orleans's winter, he had stood there watching her house window. And each time he'd seen her at the window, he'd straightened and started toward her. So she'd pulled the drapes closed and walked away. She'd almost expected to find him there in the morning. But when she'd awakened, he'd been gone. And there had been no more calls, no more attempts on his part to see her. The memory brought on another wave of hurt and longing.

"We're here, ladies," the driver announced.

"Oh my, look," Chloe exclaimed.

Shaking off her sad thoughts, Laura set her untouched champagne glass down and exited the limo. And she stepped into a winter fantasy. There on the ground at the entrance to the park were mounds and mounds of white snow. "I don't understand," she said as she walked over to join her sister and Meredith.

Kids were squealing all around her, frolicking in the mountains of white. Even the adults were laughing and carrying on like children who were seeing snow for the very first time.

Stooping down, Laura picked up a fistful of white, let it fall from her fingers. "It's snow. It's really snow," she said and when she looked up, she saw Jack. He looked so tall and handsome and wonderful standing there. But it was the look of longing and fear in his eyes that made her heart skip a beat.

"Technically, it's called artificial snow," Meredith told her. "It's made with machines called snow canons by spraying water and using air pressure—"

"I'll take it from here, Meredith," Jack said as he approached her.

She shot a glance at Meredith and her sister. "You knew about this?"

Chloe made a show of being fascinated with the snow. Meredith smiled and said, "I actually made two deals yesterday. One with Hawke Industries for business and one with Jackson Hawke personally."

"You may have to give a refund on that last one," Laura told her, still not sure she was willing to trust him with her heart again.

"All I guaranteed him was that I'd get you here so you could listen to what he has to say. I told him getting you to believe him was up to him," Meredith said. "But personally, Laura, I'd listen.

I've made enough matches to know when two people have found something special. It would be such a shame to walk away from that without being absolutely sure."

"All I'm asking for is ten minutes, Laura," Jack said. "Listen to what I have to say and if you still can't forgive me and want me out of your life, I'll sign over the Contessa to you and never bother you again."

A part of her was afraid to listen. She was afraid because she wanted to believe that what they'd shared had been real and that she would fall for more lies now.

"Please, Laura. Ten minutes. It's all I ask."

"All right," she said.

"This way," he told her and led her through the gates of the park to a waiting horse and carriage.

"I don't understand," she said as he helped her into the carriage where he settled them both under a bright red throw and nodded for the driver to leave. "How did you manage this? The park is closed to all vehicles. It's walking tours only since Hurricane Katrina."

"Meredith arranged it. And the snow," he told her.

The horse's hooves made a clip-clopping sound as the carriage drove along the winding path through the huge oaks glittering with white lights. Everywhere she looked, there were mounds and mounds of white snow lining the paths, turning the park into a winter wonderland. "But why?"

"Because that night you took me to see the lights, you told me about your snow-deprived childhood here."

That he had remembered softened something inside her, made Laura hope. And because she felt herself weakening, she made a point of looking at her watch. "Seven minutes."

"I also remembered you telling me about thinking the carousel was enchanted. Unfortunately, Meredith couldn't come up with a way to arrange that so quickly."

Laura remained silent; she was moved that he had remembered what she'd told him. As the horse continued on its way amid more snow, she said, "All of this… It must have cost a fortune."

"I considered it a small price to pay to get you here."

When they reached the Carousel Gardens, the horse stopped and Jack said, "I thought we'd walk from here."

They exited the carriage and when Jack helped her down, he held on to her for several seconds. When she stepped back, he released her. For the next few minutes, he said nothing and when they reached the Carousel House, they stopped.

"I got the letter telling me about the donation you made to restore the carousel in memory of my grandfather." She turned to him then and asked the question that had plagued her. "Why did you do that, Jack?"

"I made the donation after you took me here. I could see how much that carousel meant to you. And you taking me here, sharing it with me, meant a lot to me. I think it's when I fell in love with you."

Laura looked away, wanting to believe him, afraid, too. "If you loved me, how could you use me the way you did?"

"I didn't."

"I heard what you told Matt. I heard the way you told him, about us making love, about how he was the loser now because you'd taken me from him." Even now, the memory of his words made her feel raw inside.

"I never meant to hurt you, Laura. It was anger and years of bitterness that caused me to say those things."

"If you're saying you didn't know about me and Matt, I don't believe you."

He frowned and she thought she could detect a trace of temper as he insisted, "I *didn't* know about the two of you. At least not at first. And I'll admit that when I found out and we made that bet, I did think about seducing you to get back at him. But that plan lasted about a minute because as hard as I tried to convince myself that I was pursuing you because of Matt, it didn't work. Matt was the last thing on my mind when we were together." He caught her by the shoulders, turned her to face him. "He was the last thing on my mind when I kissed you, when I held you, when I made love to you. Because I fell in love with you, Laura."

"Then why didn't you tell me about Matt being your stepbrother after we became lovers? Why let me think you didn't even know him?"

"I wanted to tell you. I started to tell you that night in my hotel suite. But then you were upset about losing the hotel and were insisting you pay off on our bet. I wanted you so badly that night and then once we made love, I was afraid to tell you because you would think that I'd used you. I also was afraid that Matt would come through with the money to pay off the note and I would lose you to him."

"You should have trusted me, Jack."

"Yes, I should have. But at the time, I was in a panic. All I could think of was that I didn't want to lose you to him the way my father had lost my mother to Peterson's father."

"I'm not your mother, Jack. And you're not your father."

"Don't you think I realize that now?" he demanded. "I'm sorry I hurt you. I'd sooner cut my heart out than hurt you. Don't you think if I could take it all back, take all those horrible things I said back that I would?"

"I don't know, would you?" she asked, but she already knew the answer, Laura admitted as she felt her heart lighten.

"Yes, I would, dammit. But I can't. All I can do is tell you that I love you. And hope that you still love me enough to give me another chance. Will you give me another chance?"

Laura heard the plea in his voice, saw the care shining in his eyes. She slid her arms around his neck, and, smiling up at him, she said, "Yes, I'll give you another chance, Jackson Hawke, because I love you, too."

Epilogue

December, one year later.

When the car turned onto the exit for City Park, Laura looked over at her husband and said, "Jack, I thought we were going to dinner."

"We are. But there's a little stop we need to make first," he told her as the car pulled to a stop at the entrance to City Park.

After Jack helped her ease her very pregnant body from the vehicle, Laura couldn't help but notice there were no lines stretched around the block to view the lights in the oaks as there normally would be just days before Christmas. "Please tell me you didn't rent the park just for us."

"Only for an hour," he assured her as he led her to the gate.

"But it's Christmas, Jack. The children—"

"Will see the lights for free tonight. Everyone will. It's part of the deal I worked out with the park. But there's something I want to show you first."

"Another surprise?"

"Yes," he told her and, cupping her chin, he brushed his lips against hers.

In the ten months since she'd married Jack, her life had been filled with one surprise after another. After funding the initial improvements for the Contessa, Jack had turned over the hotel to her completely. He hadn't interfered or offered advice unless she'd requested it. She'd implemented her marketing plans and the Contessa was doing remarkably well. Her marriage to Jack had proved equally surprising. They had merged their lives, as well as their hearts. He sought her opinions, shared his thoughts and feelings with her as she never dreamed he would. While his relationship with his mother and stepfamily remained strained, the bitterness seemed to have waned and he'd grown more comfortable being part of her family.

To her surprise the passion between them remained just as powerful now as it had a year ago—despite her watermelon-size belly. But it had been the life growing in her belly that had come as the biggest surprise. She wasn't sure who was more thrilled about the baby—her or Jack. What she was sure of was that she had never felt more loved or cherished or happy in her life.

"Good evening, Mr. Hawke. Mrs. Hawke," the clerk at the gate said.

"Evening," Jack said. "Everything ready?"

"Yes, sir. Everything's ready."

"This way, Mrs. Hawke," Jack told her.

Rather than surprised, Laura was deeply touched by the sight of the horse and carriage. After Jack assisted her into the carriage and covered her with a throw, she rested in the comfort of his arms as the driver took them through the park. The horse and carriage made its way along the winding path through the oaks glittering with white lights. Laura couldn't help remembering a similar ride with Jack in the park last December and her shock to discover he'd had snow pumped along the roads to give her the white Christmas she'd dreamed of as a child. A gust of wind whipped through the trees and set the lights to shivering. Laura shivered, too, and burrowed under the blanket closer to Jack.

"If you're too cold, we can go back," Jack offered.

"No, I'm fine. It's just the humidity," she explained to him. "It makes it seem colder than it is."

When they reached the Carousel Gardens, the carriage stopped and Jack helped her from the carriage. He frowned and looked up at the sky. "I swear it's dropped ten degrees since we got here. And if I didn't know any better, I'd swear those were snow clouds."

"I wish," she said and she did. Snow in New Orleans was a rare thing indeed.

"You sure you're not too cold?"

"Quit fussing, Hawke, and show me the surprise."

Taking her hand, Jack led her down the path toward the Carousel House. As they made their way to her favorite part of the park, Laura felt another wave of love for the man she'd married. Thanks to Jack's donation, the antique carousel that she adored was on its way to being fully restored. Unfortunately, the expertise needed and painstaking detail could not be rushed. As a result, the carousel was still inoperable for this holiday season.

When they turned the corner, Laura heard the music and smiled at the familiar sound. "The calliope is working."

"Yes," he told her and guided her along the next curve of the path.

And then she saw it. Her beloved carousel aglow with lights, music playing, horses weaving up and down as it turned in a circle. "But I thought it wasn't finished. The restorer said it would be another month," she exclaimed.

"They managed to finish ahead of schedule," Jack told her.

Laura looked at her husband. "How? By working around the clock?"

Jack's cheeks darkened slightly. "Trust me, they were well compensated. Wait here a second," he told her and hopped onto the carousel. After disappearing inside the maze of mirrors for a moment, the carousel slowed to a stop. Returning to her, he offered his hand and said, "Come on."

He helped her up onto the carousel and once she was on, she went straight to Pegasus and lovingly stroked the horse. "It must have cost you a fortune to do all this."

"It was a small price to pay to see that look on your face. Do you like it?" he asked.

"I love it. And I love you, Jackson Hawke," she said, wrapping her arms around his neck.

"Not half as much as I love you, Mrs. Hawke," he responded and covered her mouth with his. When he slid his hands down her body, cupped her bottom and pulled her to him, Laura thrilled at the feel of his arousal. Knowing that he wanted her so much even now fed her own hunger for him.

Another blast of wind sent her scarf and coat whirling around her and Jack ended the kiss. He tugged the scarf around her neck and there was no mistaking the love and desire in his eyes as he looked at her. "I think I'd better get you out of this cold, Mrs. Hawke," he said.

But Laura barely heard him as she spied the white flakes beginning to fall. Surprised and delighted, she said, "Jack, look. It's snowing."

"I'll be damned," he said, laughter in his voice. Scooping her up into his arms, he stepped off the carousel and began walking back to the carriage. "Looks like you're going to finally get your Christmas fairytale," he told her.

Oh, but she'd gotten so much more than her Christmas fairytale, Laura thought as she reached up and brushed snow from his brow. She'd gotten the whole fairytale when she'd gotten Jack's love.

* * * * *